Spearfinger

Spearfinger
Carl Spaberg, Ace Reporter
Vol. 1

Rob Smales

Bad Ideas Press

First Edition, Bad Ideas Press, October 2023

ISBN

978-1-959271-02-4

---

1. https://selfpubbookcovers.com/Unique_Digital

For Scott, Dan, and Dave, board members of the New England Horror Writers and editors for Wicked Creatures. *This one's kind of your fault, you guys. Thanks for that. And for Shannon, who listens to me babble so much about what I'm doing, even without reading the stories she probably knows them better than I do.*

Special thanks go out to Mellisa Sherlin, Tim Krikorian, and Johanna Frappier for providing excellent feedback right when I was looking for it, with extra thanks for Tim and his brother Steve for providing title advice—they're the reason no one has to look at the cover of this thing and try to pronounce U'tlun'ta.

MONDAY

It Begins

They all screamed like children.

The thought floated through Ron's mind as he scrabbled at the dirt and gravel, packed nearly hard as tarmac by the passage of backhoe and dump truck. Both machines sat in the site, and he could have driven the truck out of there, but he'd gone right past it in his headlong sprint, reduced to blind, panicked flight.

Construction was a hard job, and one of the things it built was hard men, especially Ron's crew. No shit. Cal had once, in a moment of distraction, punched a drywall screw right through the meat of his hand, then, without comment or complaint, backed the screw out, wrapped the hand in a rag, and kept working. Dave had gone three days on a broken foot, merely tightening his bootlaces for support, before they'd forced him to go to the doctor. All five had stories like that; times they'd sucked it up and driven on, because *that's what you do.*

But Joe, Matt, Cal, even Dave, they'd all wailed like little boys in the end. And Ron, who'd never run from a fight in his life, even that time it had been three-on-one during dollar beer night at The Tap, had lit out as fast as he could while his friends—hell, his *crew*—died behind him. He'd almost made it to the road, might have gotten away, but he'd stepped in a hole, felt something snap in his ankle, and—

Thunder boomed, so loud and close the ground shook. Ron looked back, tear-streaked eyes wide—and relaxed. He spoke a single word, confused even amidst this struggle for his life.

"Mom?"

"No," Mom whispered.

Then Ron also screamed like a child, under the clear, sunny sky.

TUESDAY

The Boss of Me

Carl burst into the outer office, ignored the boss's current PA, and marched toward Max's door. Without even looking up, the young lady—*Julia*, Carl was pretty sure, and he had a newsman's memory for names—said, "Go on in. He's expecting you."

Carl's stride faltered. *Dammit!* he thought. *So much for the element of surprise. Too late to stop now, though.* He lifted his chin to a degree that screamed *indignation*, and burst into the inner office.

"Max! I—"

"Carl." Max sat behind the desk, big office chair leaned back to a ludicrous degree, ankles casually crossed atop the blotter, hands folded behind his head. "Been expecting you. Please—" He indicated the visitor's chair with a deeply dimpled chin. "—take a seat."

The chin always threw Carl. He never forgot a face—what good reporter did?—and when he'd first come to *The Weekly World Mirror* a year ago, Max Beerman's chin had been, much like the rest of him, wholly unremarkable. Then Max had taken a one-month recovery—excuse me, *vacation*—and *boom*: it was like someone had grafted the lower half of Kirk Douglass's face onto Beerman's head. It was off-putting. It was jarring. It was . . . startlingly effective in altering one's perception of the tabloid's editor-in-chief. Things said in his somewhat smug, somewhat laughing, *I'm just enjoying the hell out of life* way

3

suddenly carried more weight. Beerman knew it, too, calling attention to the feature time and again.

The bastard.

"I want to talk to you about—"

"Take a seat, Carl." Beerman repeated the gesture with his surgically-crafted secret weapon. "Please."

"Dammit!"

Carl flounced into the chair, realized this was not the most aggressive move to make while attempting to browbeat his boss, and set his feet on the floor, leaning forward imperiously.

"There! I'm sitting. Happy?" Max opened his mouth to reply, but Carl didn't wait.

"You've got to do something about Crawley. I can't—"

"No—"

"—believe what he's—"

"—I don't."

"—trying to get away wi . . . What?"

Max's gentle smile widened. "No, I don't."

Carl's eyes bulged. "Don't you even want to hear—"

"Nope."

Indignation wasn't working. Carl shifted gears and narrowed his eyes, going for steely professionalism. "Well, you're gonna. That man down there—"

"Is your immediate superior."

Carl took a breath, re-narrowed his eyes, ignored the chin, and started again.

"That man down there is ordering me—*ordering* me—to Cherokee, North Carolina, to look into a quintuple homicide. It's the middle of nowhere, the cops have already solved it, and *it's the middle of nowhere*!" He sat back with folded arms, accidentally slipping back into *indignant*.

"Contrary to popular opinion, you *are* a reporter." Max somehow flexed his dimple, the ruthless son of a bitch. "And that sounds like news to me. Your editor says to cover it, you cover it. Case closed."

"I'm the best reporter in *Boston*! The best you've ever *seen*! It took me about five minutes' work online to *look into* this. Cherokee's in the Qualla Boundary—reservation land—so it was investigated by feds, not some bumbling local outfit. A crew clearing land for a strip mall was hit by some eco-terrorists—we can't call them that, or all the John and Jane Qs will think of bombs and planes and get all confused, so they'll be called an *ecologically conscious group* or some other bullshit—said eco-terrorists to be named later, probably once the tree huggers realize that unless they come forward and *claim* credit, they won't get any. Boom. Done. It's looked into. I can write something up about it if you want, maybe do a follow-up once those friends-of-the-forest chuckleheads give us a name, but—"

"But Crawley wants boots on the ground. Your boots, Cherokee, North Carolina ground. Have a nice flight."

Carl gaped, caught himself, and turned it into a slow, catlike blink. "I'm not going."

Max sighed. "Suit yourself."

"I refuse."

"Fine."

Carl stood. "Then I'm heading straight down to Crawley and telling him to give me another assignment." He started for the door, maintaining his arrogant strut though it felt a little spongy and he couldn't help thinking, *Why does this seem too easy?* His hand was actually on the knob when Max spoke up, voice jauntier than ever.

"You won't get one."

Aha! Carl whirled. "What do you mean? Of *course* I'll—"

"He's *given* you an assignment. Until you complete it to the best of your ability, you don't get another one."

Carl actually sputtered. "I'll walk out. You think I need this place? Don't be ridiculous! I'm the best reporter you've ever *seen*! I could have a job—"

"You may well be the best reporter I've ever seen," said Max, kicking his feet off the desk and leaning forward on his elbows, tone suddenly serious. "I've seen no *evidence* of that, but I'll admit the *possibility* is there."

"*Possibility*? You—"

"But what I *know* you are is the reporter who wrote that Maine story, the one about—"

Carl waved his hands. "I don't want to talk about that!"

"You were a guy on your way up. Hungry. And you stepped on your dick. You wrote a story that got you fired. A story rejected by every paper in Boston. Every paper in New England. A story only we would print." He waved a hand toward the framed front pages hanging behind him, *Weekly World Mirror* headlines shouting from the wall: *Elvis Probed Me on an Alien Vessel*; *Man Marries Sycamore (And They Have Kids!)*; *Bigfoot Found in Suburbs: He's a Homeowner, People!*

"You walked in here with that story a year ago, and here you still are: sitting in Cambridge, writing for the oldest tabloid rag in the country. You've bitched the whole time that this place is beneath you, but as far as anybody out there in the real world is concerned, this is where you belong."

Carl's fists balled. "I don't *belong* h—"

"You walk out that door"—Max chinned toward the exit—"tell all those real world folks you can't even work *here*, and I give it a month before you're just some yobbo with a blog, blabbing into the void with nobody listening."

Carl gaped again. "That's—You—I would *never*—"

He realized he felt about bloggers now the same way he'd felt about tabloids last year: he would never, *ever* stoop so low. And yet here he still was.

Shit.

Max must have seen the newshound's shoulders slump, for his lilting vocal bounce reappeared as he threw Carl a bone.

"Look, I know you want to dig yourself out of the hole, start your climb back to the big leagues. I get it. So, look at it this way: Crawley's not asking you to write up another carnivorous vole or giant centipede story. He's not asking you to fabricate *anything*, just to go out in the field and do some investigative journalism. You don't think there's a story there; your editor does. Go find one. Be the best damned reporter I've ever seen. Wow me. Wow *all* of us. Think of it as a step toward erasing the memory of that Maine fiasco. Think of it as"—he framed a headline in the air—"Ace Reporter Takes a Step in the Right Direction."

The son of a bitch has me. Carl glared. *It's got to be the chin.* He flounced back into the chair. *Fuck it—I've lost this one, but I can't go out weak.* He folded his arms and arched his brows, back ramrod straight.

"I *demand* an aisle seat!"

WEDNESDAY

Meet George

Mom had told him not to leave the yard, and George had listened.

Pretty much.

All the kids considered the vacant lot next door as kind of *George's yard*. And he *could* still see his house—when he was in the right place and nothing was in the way—so he was *practically* in his own yard.

Pretty much.

Besides, Jimmy and Johnny Balin had been with him, making a fort of scrap lumber and other junk—it might *look* like crap, but they were going to *rule* the next rock fight—until the brothers had been called in for dinner. Now it was just George, putting on some finishing touches and waiting to hear his own mother's call. He'd found an old stop sign that would work great as a shutter for the main window, opening to peg rocks through but closing when they needed to repel an attack. It'd be better with hinges, or even tied on at the top with a rope (if they could find some), but for now he crouched inside the fort, working the sign back and forth, carving a groove in the uneven dirt floor. Leaned against the wall and slid from side-to-side, it should work just fine.

He grinned. "We are gonna *rule*!"

Thunder rolled.

He peered out, saw nothing but blue in what sky he could see, and kept working.

Thunder rolled, closer this time.

He'd be fine in the fort—the roof was less holey than the walls—but Mom would want him in if it started raining. He worked the sign faster, trying for a smooth groove before he ran out of time.

"George?"

Startled, he peeked out again. Grandma Watatooka, Mom's mom, stood at the edge of the small clearing in front of the fort.

"Grandma? Mom send you to get me?"

Smiling, the old woman nodded, beckoning with one hand. The other was tucked inside her sweater, like that guy he'd seen in history books, Napoleon Boner.

He left the sign and went out to meet her. "Did you come over for dinner?" Then, as he drew near, worried about the *pretty much*: "Am I in trouble?"

"Yes."

Grandma's hand left her sweater and flashed across his vision. For a shocked moment, George thought his beloved grandmother had *slapped* him. Rather than heat and pain growing in his cheek, however, it was a sharp line across his neck. His surprised cry refused to leave his mouth, coming instead as a red splash against Grandma's suddenly gray face. Eyes wide, he reached for the pain, but everything he touched felt hot and wet. Grandma pushed him, hard, and he went over backward to fall, choking and gurgling, into the black.

Meet Kate

Standing on the porch, Kate Kanoska tried again. "George! Time for dinner!"

Nothing. No return cry of *Coming!* or *In a minute!* or even the old standard, *Aww, Mom!*

She grimaced. *He's in the lot. Probably so wrapped up in whatever he's doing he wouldn't hear if I had a bullhorn.*

But she'd specifically asked him to stay in *their* yard. She marched off the stoop and across the grass. *Eight's old enough to be embarrassed by Mom fetching him in front of his friends, but them's the breaks. Maybe next time he'll listen.*

She stalked along paths tramped down in the rough, not wanting to trip over any detritus hidden in the weeds and tall grass (*honestly, the kids shouldn't even play here*), calling his name. The lot wasn't very big, but it was *so* overgrown, and—

It wasn't like the movies, where someone lying on the ground is momentarily taken for napping; Kate knew something was wrong the instant she saw her son sprawled before a cobbled-together clubhouse at the base of the only good-sized tree. He was too loose, too boneless, too *wrong*. But it wasn't until she saw his throat—his flung-back head spreading the wound wide as a screaming mouth—and his side—one pale rib jutting skyward, the gash rimmed with loose strings of meat and gristle, some jerked so loose as to touch the grass beside him—that she began to scream.

Meeting the Chief

Ace reporter Carl Spaberg blended into the background, watching guys in FBI windbreakers confer over the small, broken body. This was not the trip he'd expected.

Things were shaping up!

A hand appeared from his right—someone had slipped up in his blind spot, dammit. A finger tapped the press card hanging from his breast pocket.

"I know everybody at the *One Feather*."

The white ID, along with a charcoal suit and some judicious body positioning, had gotten him past the crime scene tape; he'd never actually *said* he was with the feds. The hicks dressed as cops had simply assumed. Then he'd just kept to himself and tried to look like he belonged. And now this.

"You here from the *Cherokee Scout*?"

Carl read the man's badge and put on the big smile. "Chief Tuckwa? Carl Spaberg. Good to meet you."

Cherokee Tribal Police Chief Charlie Tuckwa's dark eyes were hard, and grew harder with a better look at Carl's press ID. "*Weekly World Mirror*? Didn't take you vultures long. You came all the way here way for this?" He threw a thumb toward the road. "No press, Mr. Spaberg. Out."

"Oh, I didn't come for this." They were zipping the child into a body bag. "I came for that construction thing the other day. Five men working the foundation of a new strip mall, massacred there at the site? Right up our alley. It's like they say, Chief: *if it bleeds, it leads*." Calling the Cherokee cop *Chief* may have been a racial slur; Carl wasn't sure. But he'd felt a dirty thrill when the word had popped out of his mouth.

If he didn't want the nickname, he should have stayed a beat cop.

"Mall site's miles from here," said the chief. "And George was eight. He didn't work construction."

Carl indicated the patchwork fort. "That there begs to differ. But that's not what got me here. Heard something while I was waiting at the Hertz counter over at Asheville Regional, this weird thing the medical examiner found. That construction crew? All five bodies were recovered *sans* livers."

Waiting for his rental, he'd have cheerfully let the call go to voicemail had he known it was Crawley, but the tricky old bastard had shown up as *UNKNOWN CALLER*. Carl was pissed to find his editor on the line, then pissed again that the old zombie had dug up something Carl himself had not—though that ancient fuck hadn't had to take any time away from *his* investigation to get to Logan and fly more than nine hundred miles, had he? But even Carl had to admit the old man had given him a delicious little factaroonie to drop on Chief Chief, here. Watching Tuckwa's expression made Crawley's involvement almost worth it.

Almost.

To be fair, the chief had that *cop face* thing down cold, but a little light went out of his eyes at the mention of the livers; it was like reading a billboard for any well-trained investigator.

"My first thought was some sort of cult thing." Which was what Carl had daydreamed about all the way to Cherokee: uncovering a death cult operating out here was the kind of thing that just *might* propel Carl Spaberg back into the big leagues—or, at least, into mainstream media.

Tuckwa finally stirred. "I still don't see what—"

"But right in the middle of my drive over here—beautiful drive, by the way, nice countryside, have you seen it?—a new homicide went out on the wire. I came to check it out. You know what I learned when I got here?"

Cop face. Carl suspected his smile was bothering the chief, so he grinned wider.

"Whoever killed little Georgie Kanoska cut his throat and took his liver. *Took his liver*. Weird, huh?"

Without a word, the chief grasped him under the arm, firmly walking him back toward the police tape perimeter.

"That seems like a connection, Chief. I can walk on my own, if you—No? Okay. Look, I know the feds are *actually* investigating here, but your office has a good reputation for cooperating with the press, and—"

The chief's voice was flat. "My office will cooperate with the press to the extent they are able."

"Chief?"

An ancient man stood with the local cops just outside the tape, bronze face weathered, hair cut in the traditional Cherokee topknot. He glanced at Carl, then focused on Tuckwa.

"*U'tlun'ta*, Chief Tuckwa."

Carl blinked. "Beg pardon?"

Lifting the fluttering plastic strip, Tuckwa shoved Carl under and out, looking at the officers manning the perimeter. "Boys? Let me introduce Mr. Carl Spaberg. Look at his face. Learn it. Carl's a tabloid reporter, here to make a buck off our local tragedy. C'mon, Thomas. Let's get you out of here." The chief took the old man's arm and began helping him toward the Kanoska house. Carl didn't think the assistance was entirely for the old man's benefit—he seemed to move just fine, and he'd gotten out there on his own.

"What's, *yoot-loon* . . . Hey, what was that?"

"U'tlun'ta," old Thomas called over his shoulder. "Beware the thunder."

Carl squinted. "Chief? What's he talking about?"

The chief didn't turn. "He's an old man. He says things."

"I thought your office cooperated with the press!"

"My *office* will." The two were almost out of sight. "Give them a call, Mr. Spaberg. Make an appointment."

And they were gone.

Fssst and Clink

Carl pulled a Heineken from the ice, thrusting another bottle in before the chips could settle. The room's little bucket only allowed two beers to chill at a time. This was okay, though. Slowed him down. His old man had always said warm beer was for shitty high school parties; Carl tended to agree.

So here I am in Cherokee, North Carolina, he thought, gazing through the window overlooking the motel parking lot. *Terrific.*

So far as he could see, the whole town—and it wasn't even a town, according to Wikipedia, merely a mountainous twelve-square-mile CDP—was just the touristy stretch where Routes 441 and 19 met, with rural residential areas sprinkled wherever people wanted to be and the Oconaluftee river running through the whole thing. And touristy meant *extra* touristy, with places like Black Bear Souvenirs, Minnetonka Moccasins, and the Tomahawk Mini-Mall. Rather than the Great Smokies Inn or the Buckshot Cabins, Carl had checked into the Super 8 on 441.

Crappy, but at least he knew what to expect

With a *fssst* and *clink*, the bottlecap landed in the wastebasket as he sat to peruse the file again. He'd made a note to find the local federal number to call—the Qualla Boundary was a jurisdictional tangle between tribal cops, the State Bureau of Investigations, and the Bureau of Indian Affairs, and he had no idea who was actually in charge of the local BIA—but he *had* called the chief's office. Officer Nelawe was as cold as her boss, but at least over the phone he hadn't had to deal with the stare. She'd said she'd check the chief's schedule and get back to him, but a couple of hours later, another officer dropped off a hastily slapped-together press release on the Kanoska case. Carl hadn't told Nelawe where he was staying; he chalked it up to Chief Tuckwa not wanting *The Mirror* in his office, and letting Carl know he knew where the reporter was.

Subtle intimidation? Nice try, small town. Carl shrugged, back burnered the thought, and turned to the press packet.

According to the release, Katherine Kanoska had told George to stay in their yard, but admitted he tended to see the boundaries of *their yard* as a little flexible. She'd seen him once or twice with a couple of friends—they were minors, thus remained unnamed, but it'd be easy enough to find out; how many neighbors could the Kanoskas have? She'd called him in at quarter to five, a little early because of the thunder.

Statements taken from the two unnamed boys and their mother corroborated the boys had been with George, building a fort, until they were called in for dinner, just before 4:30.

Katherine Kanoska made dinner early because of thunder.

His mind's ear heard old Thomas, back at the crime scene: *Beware the thunder.*

Did I *hear thunder at all today?* He couldn't remember. Could have happened while he was driving, though, listening to the radio. There'd been blue skies all day, but that didn't mean much in mountain country; thunder might roll along a ridge for miles to be heard by people who wouldn't see a drop of rain or even a cloud in the sky.

He checked the National Weather Service, but found no storm activity anywhere in this part of the state. After a moment, he picked up the phone.

"Chief's office."

"Officer Nelawe? Spaberg here."

"Terrific."

Her voice was flat and sarcastic. Despite that, Carl grinned. She sounded cute. He poured on his version of charm. "I know you're all busy playing step-and-fetch for the feds in *their* homicide investigation and all, so I'll be brief.

"Yes?"

"Did you or any of your officers hear any thunder this afternoon?"

He waited while she either mentally called for the strength to deal with him or gave the question serious thought. He hoped the latter.

"I didn't, but I'll ask around."

"Thank you, Offic—."

She hung up. He tipped his bottle toward the phone, then emptied it in two swallows.

Beware the thunder, the old guy said. Katherine Kanoska heard thunder, but I didn't, Nelawe didn't, and I'll bet she turns up a goose egg asking around.

He pulled a cold beer loose, thrusting another in its place.

Mystery thunder. Missing livers. What the hell is going on around here?

Fssst. Clink. He took a long pull.

I find that *out, and it just* might *be a step toward getting out of the tabloid shithole. This seems to be turning into something, and here I am at ground zero. Hooray for me!*

He moved to take another pull, but paused.

And how the hell did Crawly know there was more to this story?

THURSDAY

Meet Lily

The Soco's chuckle filtered through the trees, the creek a rushing undercurrent to the night song of crickets and spring peepers out looking for love. Normally, Lily would have saved the battery, but she'd caught her rod on enough underbrush along the path that frustration had forced her to turn her headlamp on. The rod was a new Pflueger ultralight—she'd saved her own money, from birthdays and such, then pestered Dad into taking her to River's Edge for it—strung with 2-lb monofilament which tangled in the leaves something fierce. She'd left before dawn, planning to surprise Dad with fresh fish for breakfast. It had been just the two of them the past couple of years, and little surprises like this had gained importance. At the sudden roll of thunder, she quickened her pace; fishing across sunrise was usually best, but rain seemed to make the trout crazy, snapping at anything and everything in a sort of feeding frenzy. And a little rain falling across the sunrise?

She couldn't wait to see Dad's face when she showed up with a stringer of fresh rainbow deliciousness.

A second roll of thunder sounded, closer, and she worried a moment that she hadn't brought a slicker, but pushed the thought aside. It was spring, which was why all the crickets and peepers were out, and—

But the amorous bugs and frogs had gone quiet during that last rumble, leaving the predawn darkness heavy and silent.

Crack!

Lily slowed. The night song's disappearance was weird, and that snapping twig had been close. She could see no farther than the trees right around her though, her LED's bright glow leaving everything beyond an impenetrable black.

Jeez—it'd be dim, but I could see farther by just moon and starlight!

Besides, the headlamp made her feel spotlit all of a sudden, visible for miles. Her flesh crawled with the paranoid certainty there was something out there, watching. She snapped the lamp off—plunging her light-adjusted gaze into deep darkness.

Crap.

She opened her eyes wide, but it didn't help; only time would bring her night vision back. She bit her lip, wishing the thin, whippy fishing rod were something more substantial—like Dad's hunting rifle, maybe—and that the frogs and crickets would come back, the familiar sound telling her the dark forest was as safe as it had always been. Her skin felt tight, almost tingling as she stretched every nerve to catch the slightest *peep* or *chirp*, but the air carried nothing but the quiet burble of the nearby creek, the loamy musk of underbrush, and the sweet smell of pine.

Crack.

That was really close. Screw it. Seeing a little would be better than nothing at all. She snapped the headlamp on—and a figure blocked the trail, not ten feet ahead.

With a shout, Lily backpedaled, heeled a root, and went down hard on her butt, Pflueger flying off into the underbrush. She got up on her palms and soles, ready to set a land speed record in the backward crab walk.

"Lily?"

She *knew* that voice—heard it in her dreams sometimes, the times she woke in tears, cut by a sense of loss freshly sharpened on the whetstone of memory. But she wasn't dreaming now. Was she? She focused the light on the figure, illuminating it from toes to shoulders—*familiar* shoulders—face still lost in shadow.

"M-Mom?"

The figure stepped forward and her mother's face, a face she hadn't seen in two years, came into the light. No—more than two; this woman was smiling, whole and healthy, without the mark of the cancer that had chewed away better than sixty pounds, leaving Lily and her dad a human skeleton to remember before it had stolen her away forever.

Or so they'd *thought*.

"M-Mom? Is that . . . is that really you?"

Her mother squatted, right hand behind her back, left stretching forth to stroke Lily's cheek, then take her chin between thumb and forefinger—a thumb and forefinger as cold and hard as marble.

"No."

The figure's right hand shot high. Lily had an instant to register the long blade gleaming in her LED's brilliant white light before it came down.

There was a gasp. A gurgle. A fresh hot copper scent mingled with the loam and pine.

Thunder rolled. Faded.

The headlamp cast its bubble of light against the dark as Lily, alone and unmoving, lay upon the trail as the song of crickets and peepers rose to mix with the creek sound once more.

ReConstruction

Carl scooped up a palmful of sandy soil and let it trickle between his fingers, watching the wind pull the trickle into skeins and dust devils dancing across the construction site.

The crime scene.

Reconstructing what had happened was simple, up to a point.

The backhoe sat on the gravel ramp into the excavation, bucket swung sideways against the pit wall across from where, according to the tools lying abandoned in the photos he'd seen, two men had been shoring up the soft soil with waling so they could eventually pour the foundation. Even Carl could see shoring was necessary: right beside where the two had been, a four-foot-high section of pit wall had collapsed, a couple hundred pounds of soil spilling onto the excavation floor. Up beside the pit, the dump truck sat, half full of dirt and rocks; in the photos, both doors had been open like stubby wings.

So, Carl thought. *A regular day: two guys in the pit, one in the backhoe, two in the truck, all five present and accounted for.*

And then it went haywire. According to the photos and diagrams he'd gotten from *The One Feather*, *The Smokey Mountain Times*, and *The Sylva Herald*—those Barney Fife cops might be obstructive, but the local Podunk press was *so* helpful to real reporters—one man was found in the pit, right there with his tools. The other pit man lay toward the top of the ramp, footprints showing he'd been running like hell. Abrasions on hands and face indicated he'd been taken down from behind. The same could be said for each of the other three, scattered in a rough dotted line all the way to the road. And that, according to a footprint and blood pattern analysis, was the order of the homicides: they'd started in the pit and worked their way out, chasing the workmen down and finishing with Ron Baker, thirty-seven, up by the road.

None of which makes any sense. Carl straightened, brushing off his hands. *They weren't surrounded; they all had a chance to run. It was a small group of attackers at most, so . . . they should have hit the truck first, working their way* inward, *to the two practically trapped in that pit.* He shook his head. *Christ, even eco-terrorists do things ass-backward out here in the sticks.*

His gaze followed the dotted line of little numbered flags still planted where bodies had been found.

The first guy died right there with his tools, like he didn't see it coming. He went down, then all the others ran straight for the road . . . and were chased down from behind.

His brow furrowed.

Almost like there was one killer? Taking them out so fast none of them actually made it off the site? With a knife? Is that even possible? And then there's the kid. And the livers.

This was looking more and more like . . . what?

The police scanner clipped to his belt squawked.

"Dispatch, this is Seventeen. You better tell the chief we got another one, north bank of the Saco, just west of the United Methodist."

"Seventeen, this is Chief Tuckwa. Call my cell immediately. Clear?"

"Clear, Chief. Seventeen out."

Carl gazed thoughtfully into the excavation. "Looks like the chief is taking something off the air. Now that is . . . interesting."

He turned toward his rental to see what would happen if he punched *Cherokee United Methodist* into his GPS. That would at least send him in the right direction. He'd just keep an eye out for the flashing lights.

Ghigooie Scene

Carl watched Chief Tuckwa as the ME zipped the little body into the bag. The cop turned and started, surprised to find Carl leaning against a tree just up the trail. In that unguarded moment, before he recognized the reporter, his dark eyes bore deep sadness. They hardened quickly, but Carl caught the transition.

Looks like Chief Chief here might be burning out.

Cops and reporters had that problem in common: the stuff they saw on the job built up. They crammed it down, but the pressure, sadness, emotional whatever, only built up again, until one day something—everyone had a different trigger, you could never really tell what was going to do it—stuck a pin in their mental balloon. They blew. They quit. They retired. They moved on. A disproportionate number of cops committed suicide. Carl considered all this a good thing: it cleared out the deadwood to make room for those who could take it. Like him.

"You again?"

The chief even sounded rough. Carl grinned. Tuckwa had been chief fifteen years, and if he *was* starting to fracture, Carl wouldn't mind being around for it. Who knew *what* might spill out of the man? He gestured toward the body with his chin, a-la Max Beerman. "You knew her?"

Tuckwa kept his eyes on Carl. "There's only a couple thousand of us here, Spaberg. I know all my people, at least on sight."

"What happened, Chief? It took me a while to find my way here. None of your people seemed inclined to point the way."

Tuckwa's lips thinned; Carl was pretty sure that qualified as a satisfied smile for Chief Charlie.

"All information needs to go through—"

"Yeah, yeah. Your office." Carl nodded. "I'll call."

Tuckwa started around him.

"Another missing liver?"

The chief stopped. Glared.

"I saw, before they closed the bag. She was—" Carl tapped his own ribcage. "—like the others." The sight had finished extracting the idea that had begun percolating in his brain out at the construction site; speaking it aloud now, Carl utterly failed to mask his excitement. "Looks to me like you have a serial killer, Chi—"

"Keep your *speculations* to yourself, Spaberg. I have a homicide investigation here." Angry, Tuckwa turned away. Carl decided to poke that balloon.

"*Three* homicide investigations." Tuckwa's back stiffened. "Two of them kids. You have a real problem, Chief. Bigger than someone like you can handle. What do the feds think?"

Tuckwa stalked away. Carl watched him go, then pulled out his mobile. *No time like the present . . .*

"Officer Nelawe! Light of my life! So good to hear your voice! Yes, it's me. Yes, again. Listen, Dianne—May I call you Dianne? Right. Just one question, Officer Nelawe: I'm looking to identify a certain individual. Cherokee, about five seven, maybe a hundred twenty pounds. Traditional hairstyle and older than God's own foreskin. First name Thomas, last unknown. Sound familiar? Mm-hmm. Well, out here in Country Mouse Town it might *look* like I'm asking you to do my job for me, but back in civilization—Hello?"

He looked at the *Call Disconnected* on his screen a moment, then tucked the phone away.

Only a couple thousand people, Chief? All right. He can't be that *hard to find.*

He followed the EMTs and their sad burden back up the path toward the cars, feeling a bit like a pallbearer for this little girl he didn't know—but at least he wouldn't get lost again. Watching them maneuver the stretcher through the trees, Carl was struck by a thought.

"Working emergency services, I'll bet you boys know just about everybody around, don't you?"

FRIDAY

Meeting Kahleskawe

The sedan rode a dust cloud down the long dirt driveway. Carl rolled to a stop and stepped out, giving the area a quick scan.

"Wow. Somebody actually *lives* in this dump?"

Thomas Kahleskawe's single-wide trailer looked not so much as if it had been parked beneath the tall red maple as grown there, ancient cinderblock foundation cracked and sunken, roof thick with moss from the constant shade, small satellite dish sprouting from one corner of the green carpet like a mushroom.

Sam and Ben—not the brightest pair in the world, Carl had been happy to discover—were eager to help, once they'd gotten Lily Ghigooie's body loaded. Of course, they'd seen him talking with the chief at the scene, and, again, the charcoal suit hadn't hurt. And it wasn't *exactly* a lie that he was trying to help Chief Tuckwa; he was *trying*, Chief Chief just wasn't *letting* him. They'd given fantastic directions to this stretch of land on the outskirts of town where Carl would find the old man he now knew as *Thomas Kahleskawe*.

He slammed his car door, announcing his presence, and took his time climbing onto the rickety porch. If Kahleskawe was the nervous type, he wanted to give the old boy plenty of time to peek out and see him coming. He knocked, rapid and loud.

"Thomas Kahleskawe?"

"Open!"

The trailer's interior was dim in the shadow of the maple—about ten degrees cooler than outside, though he heard no air conditioner's hum—and smelled of old man, old beans, and old farts. Carl mouth-breathed until he realized the air even tasted foul, then shut his lips with a snap.

"I help you?"

The old man sat on a sofa even more organic looking than the trailer, a brown pile of lumps, bumps, and sinkholes, without a straight line to be seen, and the rest of the room fit right in around it—with one exception. On one wall hung, incongruously huge and modern, what had to be a fifty-inch flatscreen TV. A stubby remote stuck out of the old man's fist, the black-and-white scene paused to show a man and woman on the deck of a riverboat, sporting clothing so ostentatious Carl doubted it had ever *really* been in fashion.

Kahleskawe caught Carl staring. "*Mississippi Gambler*, nineteen-fifty-three." His voice was rusty but strong as he gestured with the remote then put it on his armrest. "A gift from my great-grandson, so he feels less guilty about not visiting. His son put in the satellite. Same reason." His eyes, which should have been black in the dim room, caught and reflected the cold silver glow from the black-and-white image on the huge screen, false blind eyes that made the back of Carl's neck tingle. "I ask again: I help you?"

"Maybe open a window?"

The old man just stared with that silver gaze. Carl sidestepped and sat on what he hoped was a chair at the end of the sofa, flinching at the stale air puffing up from the cushion. The smell, the eyes, it was all throwing him off his game. He groped for an icebreaker.

"My name's Carl Spaberg, and I'm with the *Weekly World Mirror*. I—"

"I know you. Saw you at the place she got the Kanoska boy."

She? "Yes, sir. I'm helping Chief Tuckwa to—"

"Chief don't like you much."

Carl blinked. "Uh . . . no, I guess not." This wasn't going at all the way he'd planned. "Why? Did the chief say—"

"Oh, he don't have to say he don't like you. It was in his walk. In his face. My eyes are old, Carl Spaberg, but they *see*."

Carl looked at those silver orbs again—and the black-and-white image vanished as the Roku screen saver popped onto the TV. The white reflection disappeared from Kahleskawe's eyes, leaving them just as black as Carl had expected, though somehow no less bright.

"Ah . . . Yeah. That day by the Kanoska place, you said something, Mr. Kahleskawe. *Beware the thunder*. Do you remember that?"

"I remember."

"What did you mean by that? And a moment ago, you said *she* got the Kanoska boy. Who's *she*?"

The old face was flat. "You're not working with Tuckwa. He don't like you, he don't work with you."

Carl sputtered, caught out in his lie. "Well, no, but I'm *trying* to—"

"But Tuckwa isn't asking the right questions. He's stuck under the BIA's thumb. Had lots of white man's school. Wants everything modern. No room in the world for the new things and the old things together. He would never tell me I'm a crazy old man. He was raised better. But I been around a long time, and I *see*. I see what he thinks when I talk. I also see the world is a bigger place than Charlie Tuckwa thinks. And now I see a white man, coming around behind the chief's back and asking the right questions."

He grinned, showing gums smooth as a newborn's.

"Guess maybe now, I seen everything, huh? But I'll tell you, Carl Spaberg. I'll tell you for the children. Because you ask the right questions.

"Long ago, long before white men came, there was a monster roamed these mountains, an ogre in the shape of a woman made of stone. Stone skin, stone hair, stone dress, and stone hands, with one finger"—he held up a forefinger—"long and sharp, like the head of a spear. My people called her *U'tlun'ta*, the Spearfinger, and she hunted my people with her blood-rimmed mouth."

"Sounds like she'd be easy to spot," said Carl. "Gray skin, spear finger, bloody mouth. Kind of a giveaway."

Kahleskawe nodded. "But she used her magic to change, take the shape of an old woman, someone known to the children, for it was children she desired. She would find a child, take the shape of a grandmother or a village elder, hiding her spear finger as she did so, for the spear finger was the one thing she could not change. And when the children came to her, she would strike them down with her finger and eat their livers."

"Their . . . livers?"

The old man nodded. "My people feared for their children, and so they hunted U'tlun'ta."

"Even with her shapeshifting?"

"U'tlun'ta could change how she looked, but still she was made of stone. When she walked, it sounded like thunder.

Birds took flight at her passage. The hunters looked for birds flying for no reason, listened for the sound of thunder with no rain."

Katherine Kanoska heard thunder with no rain. Son of a bitch.

"They followed the birds and thunder until they found U'tlun'ta. But her skin of stone turned aside their arrows. U'tlun'ta ate some of their livers in the night, but many of the hunters escaped. They dug a pit and covered it with leaves, then lured her to fall in. They'd filled the pit with sharp sticks, but her stone body broke them. They shot arrows, but again her stone skin turned them aside. She was trapped, but they could not harm her, and she would find a way out. Then, a chickadee appeared, and told the hunters that though U'tlun'ta had a body of stone, she held her heart in her spear finger hand to keep it safe. The hunters shot arrows into her fist, striking and stopping her heart."

Carl nodded. "The old Achilles fist."

"They refilled the pit and returned to their villages heroes, killers of the terrible U'tlun'ta."

"Okay." Carl nodded again, trying to see where the old man was going. "So, what, you think somebody's following this Yuntu . . . Yuntool . . . this Spearfinger's method or something?"

"What I think is, the story is wrong. I think they did not kill U'tlun'ta, but buried her alive, where she waited for hundreds of years, growing angrier and hungrier, until someone dug her up."

Carl squinted. "Uh-huh. And who . . . ?"

"Those construction men, digging where they should not."

Carl pictured the site; one wall partially collapsed right at the bottom of the excavation, an area almost the size of a person; the killing progressing outward rather than in, in an almost straight line from that collapse, as if whatever had emerged had—

He shook his head, clearing his mental Etch-A-Sketch. It fit, it really did, but he couldn't believe he'd almost considered it. "So, let me get this straight: You really think some monster lay buried in the earth for hundreds of years, and the other day it just up and started killing people? Wouldn't the simple answer be someone who knows the story is just—"

"I'll tell you what I told Chief Tuckwa: When I was a boy, this television from my great grandson would not have been believed. Not by Cherokee. Not by white men. You told people about it, they'd have said it was a made-up story, called you crazy."

"Well, yeah, but that's not—"

"When I was young, I worked for a white man, hauling ice for people's ice boxes. Kids today, like little Georgie Kanoska, with their electricity and their refrigerators, I tell them that, they don't believe me. Think it's a made-up story. And here I am, been alive a long time, and I know both things are true. The world is bigger than what you see every day, Carl Spaberg. Older, too. You need to open your eyes and *see*."

He turned back to the TV and picked up the remote.

"The chief's not looking for U'tlun'ta. She's not modern enough for him. You want to help the chief? Follow your eyes and ears. Look for the birds and listen for the thunder."

"One thing," said Carl. "Why kids? And why just the livers? What's up with that?"

"You want me to tell you why U'tlun'ta does what she does? I can't even tell you why my microwave always thinks it's noon."

The black-and-white world came back to the screen, and the old man's eyes went silver in the glare.

Carl let himself out.

At the Library

Carl closed *The Vampire Slayer's Field Guide to the Undead* and pushed the thick book toward the pile of similar tomes covering the other half of his table.

"Huh."

He'd wondered just how *common knowledge* the legend of U'tlun'ta was. Fresh from Kahleskawe's speech about the world having room for the new and the old, he'd decided to go a little old school himself and do some research at the library. *It's an ancient local story,* he'd thought. *They've practically got to have something on it there. And if not, someone at the library should know where to find it. Besides,* he'd finished with a grin, *why do the research myself when there's a library staff to do it for me?*

Once he'd gotten to the Qualla Boundary Public Library—a surprisingly low, flat, plain building, in Carl's opinion, for a bastion of words, but what should one expect out here in Hicksville USA—he'd found not a staff waiting to help him, but a single librarian. Ms. Oolootsa seemed to have been designed to be a librarian: tall, somewhere between forty and sixty, with a stern expression, a high-necked dress, and that *glasses on a neck ribbon* thing Carl figured must be some kind of requirement.

When he explained he was an actual newspaper reporter and showed her his press ID—finger carefully covering the words *Weekly World Mirror*—her response was better than Carl had hoped for. More and more these days, the public failed to perceive the enormity of his position as *truth teller to the masses,* reserving their excitement for the folks from the *television* news, as if they somehow did something more, or better. Most TV news personalities weren't even the actual reporters doing the job, but *news presenters*: good-looking talking heads who just read what other people put in front of them.

As a serious guardian of the written word, the librarian apparently thought a lot more of news *papers* than news *programs*, and her excitement at his presence was a welcome surprise. And she *definitely* knew her job, inundating him with books once he'd made clear what he was looking for, marching silently off between the stacks and returning again and again. And again. Spearfinger was apparently this region's favorite bogey, almost as popular to the Cherokee here as Bigfoot was in Washington state. She was mentioned in everything from little tourist brochures found in the visitor's center to that three-inch-thick doorstop he'd just pushed aside, a kind of overview of monster legends from around the world. Hell, there was even a Spearfinger bike trail on nearby Fire Mountain. He'd probably have a harder time finding someone local who'd *not* heard the story of the liver-lunching ogress.

Have to give the old boy credit on one thing: he's right, these killings are a match for the old legend. The adults don't quite fit, but fort-building kid and fishing girl are a perfect match. A serial killer refining his MO? Do they do *that?*

"Can I help you find anything else?"

Ms. Oolootsa appeared at his elbow, looming tall, her whisper loud in the otherwise silent library, startling Carl out of his thoughts.

"Christ! Someone should put a bell on you. I, uh . . ." He looked at the untidy heap he'd shoved aside and felt her also studying the pile with quiet disapproval.

She's a librarian, he thought. *Did she think she* wouldn't *be putting books away?* Besides, he planned to add *one* more book to the pile.

"I don't suppose you have anything that looks at the whole Spearfinger thing from a, uh, *religious* point of view? Like a Cherokee bible or a torah, something like that?"

She shook her head. "No, but everyone around here knows *something* of U'tlun'ta. The older they are, the more they know. Years ago, I would have told you to talk to Marianne Tuckwa. She was a *didanawisgi,* and knew more than most. But she died years ago. Her grandfather is still with us, but—"

"I'm sorry?" Carl set his phone on the table, voice recording app running to capture their words. "She was a dee-dana-whatnow?"

The tall woman looked surprised, then pleased, and leaned down toward the recording device, enunciating a little self-consciously. "Didanawisgi. Dee-dan-a-wiz-gi. Medicine woman. She was old, and knew much, and may have had what you're looking for, but passed away a few years ago."

"She was old and her *grandfather's* still around?"

She almost smiled. "Thomas Kahleskawe remembers when people got around in horse-drawn wagons and buggies."

Wait—What?

"Kahleskawe? Lives just outside of town? Looks older than God's own—uh, I mean, very old? *That* Thomas Kahleskawe?"

"There's only one."

"Okay, yes. I just came from his trailer. He's the one who turned me on to all this Spearfinger stuff in the first place."

The librarian shrugged. "Then it sounds like you probably got the best version of the story you're likely to get. Thomas Kahleskawe didn't learn this stuff from a book. He learned from his father, who learned from his father, and on down the line. He was didanawisgi before Marianne, and has forgotten more about the old ways than most people around here ever know." She sighed. "Probably literally."

"What do you mean by that?"

She shrugged again, glancing at his phone. Carl nodded. As much as some people liked feeling important, having someone listen so closely to them—especially someone from the press—many were uncomfortable going on-record when talking shit about someone, especially someone they knew, or would see every day. *Was* she looking to talk shit about Kahleskawe?

Only one way to find out.

He picked up the phone, made a few swipes across the screen, and set it face down to the other side of the table, away from Ms. Oolootsa, then held his hands high, a magician with nothing up his sleeves.

"Off the record."

All he'd really done was swipe the recording app into the background and lock his screen; the phone was still catching every word.

"Well . . ." She pursed her lips. "Thomas is *old*. We don't know *how* old because he doesn't have a birth certificate. He claims he was born before white folks started what he calls *all that foolishness.*"

"Before birth certificates?" *Haven't we always had those?* "When *did* we white folks start all that foolishness?"

"Birth certificates? Around 1905 or 1910, something like that. But they probably weren't too diligent about keeping track of Cherokees for a while. Maybe nineteen-teens or twenties for us, I'd guess."

"Wait—so, you're ballparking his age at anywhere from a hundred to a hundred-twenty? I figured him for his seventies."

This time she *did* smile. "My Grandma remembered Thomas being all grown up when she was a little girl. He's like a time traveler. You ever watch a movie or something set in the free love seventies or rocking fifties? Or even the roaring twenties?"

"Of course."

"Those aren't just movies for Thomas. They're memories. He was there, seeing and doing things. And he remembers it all—or, he did. Until recently."

"Recently?"

"He's started . . . slipping the past few years. Physically, he doesn't seem near his stated age, but his mind wanders."

"Really? He seemed pretty sharp to me."

Carl's mouth was moving on automatic; make the right sounds at the right times, he knew, and the interviewee would keep talking—and if you didn't actually know what to ask, letting them free-associate and ramble was not a bad way to let them say the wrong thing and hang themselves. Or someone else. His mind was processing at high speed. He'd formed a conclusion he liked and was now looking to support it. It might not have been the scientific method, but that didn't matter: he wasn't in search of good science, but a good *story*. The story was everything, and the juicier the better.

We've definitely got a serial killer out here—a Native American serial killer for sure, maybe the first ever, mimicking the legendary killings of a local myth, practically this region's Paul Bunyan. And who's the local expert on all things Spearfinger? The oldest guy in the county—hell, maybe the oldest guy in the country—and he just happens to be losing his marbles.

Coincidence? Who cares?

"He hides it pretty well," Ms. Oolootsa was saying. "You have to get to know him, talk to him awhile, and it starts to show, I guess. That's what people say, anyway—I don't spend a lot of time with him myself."

"He hides it? So, he's aware of it?"

"I think he must be."

"And he doesn't like it? It upsets him?"

She shrugged again. "Probably. I mean, I'd be upset if it was happening to *me*, so . . ."

So I could play the loopy and *angry cards.*

He stood without warning, startling the librarian.

"Thank you, Ms. Oolootsa. You've been more help than you know. Uh . . ." He gestured at the heap of discarded books. "You know what to do. I've got to—"

I've got to get out of here so I can pace and think, is what he really wanted to say, but he went with, "I'll call if I have any further questions." He didn't think he would, but it was just the kind of parting shot that left John and Joan Qs feeling more important than they were—and if he *did* have to come back to her, that feeling would make it easier to get her talking again.

"Certainly. I'll be here." She looked at the table. "Probably still reshelving these."

He nodded and started for the door in his best important-looking stride, but something she'd said moments ago finally managed to get his attention. He stopped, turned slowly, his brain still sluggishly churning the new idea.

"Ms. Oolootsa?"

He returned to her, walking without meaning to, not even feeling his feet on the floor.

She stopped stacking books and straightened. "Mr. Spaberg?"

"Did you say . . . Did you say the old medicine woman, Thomas Kahleskawe's granddaughter, was Marianne *Tuckwa*?"

She must have heard something in his voice, and suddenly sounded uncertain. "Yes?"

It was a good thing he'd drawn close, because his words were a whisper. "As in *Chief* Tuckwa?"

"Marianne Kahleskawe married Talking Horse Tuckwa, and they had a baby they named Charles."

He was very close now, looking slightly up to meet her gaze, but he didn't—couldn't—speak, in case it broke the spell. He merely stared at her with very wide eyes, *willing* her to go on, to actually say the words.

"So, uh . . . Yes. Marianne Tuckwa was Chief Tuckwa's mother."

"And Kahleskawe's his great-grandfather."

"Oh! Well, yes."

He blinked once. Twice.

Then his hands shot out to grip her shoulders and he planted a kiss right on her stern lips.

"*Mister Spaberg!*"

"You, Ms. Oolootsa, are a wonderful, *wonderful* woman!"

And then he was striding through the low-linteled front door, a wild grin plastered across his ecstatic face, head filled with a terrible, wonderful idea.

Fssst and Clink II

He was going to be too busy thinking to bother with swapping warm beers for cold in that ridiculous ice bucket, and warm beer was still, in his opinion, piss. He bustled into his room carrying six fresh Heinekens and eyed the sink.

No, I might need that later. Besides, using the sink as a beer cooler is seriously *low-class.*

Instead, he flung the waste basket liner into the corner and practically ran to the ice machine, trash barrel under one arm. He raced back to his room, thrust five of the bottles home in the ice, then scooped up the sixth. There was a *fssst* and he was scanning the room, bottle cap in hand, looking for the trash barrel. He spotted it on the counter, full of ice and beer, laughed, and skated the cap toward the corner where the discarded trash liner lay.

Let housekeeping earn their tip! I've got to work while it's still fresh.

He fired up his voice-recording app and started pacing the room with the phone, gesturing with the bottle between swallows.

"Okay, okay. What do we have? Well, first off, there's a serial killer—boom, that'll sell papers right there. Native American serial killer, maybe the first; that'd be a feather in my cap, if it works out. There's that Billy Glaze, but Google says the Innocence Project may have cleared him. Fingers crossed.

"What else? He started with a five-man spree, which is good, then shifted to kids, which is *better*. Did he shift to more closely mirror the Spearfinger legend? Or for some other

49

reason? Have to see what the FBI says on that. No—they're shit at sharing. I'll find my own headshrinker to weigh in. I'll . . . I'll write it both ways, see which sounds better, then maybe call Marty. He's got a sheepskin on the wall and he'll say anything to see his name in print.

"All right, players in this story? Thomas Kahleskawe, oldest man in the country—no, the world; no one can dispute it with no birth certificate, right?—local expert in Cherokee lore, grew up believing the Spearfinger legend, yadda yadda, quietly losing his marbles. Forgetting things, that's a sign of dementia, right? And dementia—"

His empty bottle *clacked* onto the counter and he thumbed a quick Google search.

"Yes! Dementia *may* cause personality changes, maybe even make a calm person aggressive. What about . . . ?"

Another search. A quick scan. Another search.

"Sweet! 'Along with cognitive decline, ninety percent of patients with dementia experience behavioral and psychological symptoms, such as psychosis, aggression, agitation, and depression.' *Psychosis*! I've hit the mother lode! It's a chain of *mights*, *maybes*, and *possibles*, but for the internet this is *solid*! Whole stars' careers have been washed down the tubes on shit weaker than this! By next week, I could have the whole country insisting we strap Tom Kahleskawe into Old Sparky and lining up to flip the switch!"

He snatched another beer from the barrel and sent the cap winging toward the corner.

"But wait! There's more! We have local top cop, Chief Charlie Tuckwa, assisting the feds with local knowledge and manpower. Does he know old man Kahleskawe? You bet your ass! The old man's his great-grandfather! Does he know about Kahleskawe's mental deterioration? You bet your ass—see above! But does he bring the old man in for questioning? Bring him up to the feds? Look into him at all? Of course not! Why? *Because the old man's his great-grandfather*! He's even spotted—by this *impeccable* reporter, no less—escorting Kahleskawe away from one of the scenes! Could it be—*gasp*—a cover-up? It's possible. Hell, by the time I'm done with this, Chief Charlie himself might think he's guilty."

He downed the rest of the beer and slapped the second empty beside the first, mentally churning through all the assumptions he'd just made—well, everything he could remember off the top of his head, but that's why he was recording this—looking for big obvious holes.

"And holy shit, ladies and gentlemen. I don't have a shred of proof about any of this, but the whole thing is technically possible. It's *actually* possible."

Just tossing a third bottle cap toward the corner he heard a commotion in the parking lot: car doors slamming, voices calling back and forth. He nudged one curtain aside and peered out. Abby Haines, a well-known field reporter for NBC, was getting out of a van with what Carl assumed was her camera man. The shouting had apparently been a greeting between Abby and Barry Stone, reporter for the Boston Globe. Carl and Barry had exchanged words back when Carl was transitioning down to the *Mirror*. Mocking words on Barry's part. The prick.

"If NBC is sending out a field reporter rather than relying on local stringers," he said into his phone, "and Barry the prick came all the way here from Boston, then the serial killer angle must have hit the wire. They're the first of a wave. This Super 8 is about to see a *serious* surge in business. It's lucky I—"

It galled him, and if he was going to admit it, he'd do it silently; there would be no record of him saying this aloud, even just for himself.

I'm lucky Crawley sent me down here. I don't know how the old zombie knew there was an actual story, but damn me if the wrinkly bastard didn't hit the nail right on the head. I may . . . I may actually owe him for this.

He let the curtain drop, added a third empty to the counter, and caught his reflection in the mirror above it. He saw a rumpled guy in a rumpled suit who hadn't even bothered with a tie that morning, perspiring from his excited pacing, three trash can beers deep in the middle of the afternoon. They'd gone down quick, and he was starting to feel them. And it showed. He straightened his spine, neatened his collar, and ran his fingers through his hair.

Okay. Got to calm down and focus.

Barry the prick was already here, and there would be others: men and women of the press, the major papers; players in that arena he'd been ousted from before he'd been allowed to truly shine. An arena he planned to enter again. But he'd have to play it careful and do it right.

I've gotten sloppy at the Mirror. *I can't just make shit up on this one. A little fiction is okay, but I'm going to need a few facts. Any facts would be nice. The press who are going to be here—even Barry—really know their shit. Some may have been playing the game a long while, but none of them is Carl Spaberg. I've got a serious jump, here. I've seen shit they haven't—and won't. I've got a theory—a fucking awesome theory—that's possible. It might be true. Gotta go out and make it happen.*

He opened a drawer and pulled out his tie. Threading it through his collar, he began knotting it in a series of short, vicious jerks.

I think you may be running a cover-up for a serial killer, Chief Charlie. Ready or not, here I come ...

~~**~~

Of course, Officer Nelawe had no interest in telling Carl where the chief actually *was*.

"Chief Tuckwa is busy with the investigation. He's called a press conference for nine tomorrow morning at the Cherokee Cultural School Cultural Arts Center."

Carl put on his friendliest voice. "Look, Dianne, you and I both know the feds are running the investigation. The chief's just putting his face on it and talking to the locals. These other reporters, they're just getting here—hell, some of them haven't even arrived yet. Am I right? I've been here pretty much since the beginning! You and I are on a first-name basis—"

"No, we're not."

"—doesn't that make me practically a local boy?"

Silence flowed down the line for a couple of heartbeats. Three. Four.

"Chief Tuckwa's called a press conference for nine tomorrow morning at the Cultural Arts Center."

"All right, Officer Nelawe: we're not on a first-name basis. See? I gave a little. Your turn. What do you say?"

She sighed. "Chief's called a press conference tomorrow at the CAC."

"What time?"

She hung up.

"Right. So much for my charm—but I think she's weakening. Oh, well. Plan B."

If I can't get hold of one end of this investigation, there's always the other. Let Barry the prick and his merry band of Johnny-come-latelys wait for the press conference and see what Chief Big Cover-up has to say. I've got other fish to fry.

He scooped up his keys and headed for the door, on his way to a broken-down little trailer on the outskirts of town. If he couldn't talk to the chief, he could at least keep track of his personal number-one suspect.

To his relief, the parking lot was empty of people—Abby, Barry, and the camera guy were probably settling into their rooms right then. He had no desire to hear Barry's brainless babbling about how *he* was a *real* reporter, thank you very much. As he slipped behind the sedan's wheel, his stomach rumbled.

Food. Yes.

Something inside him to soak up those recent beers (in case he *did* run into the chief) and a thermos of stakeout coffee. Sitting in one place watching nothing happen for hours on end was the boring part of investigating he avoided when he could. If he was going to try to keep an eye on Kahleskawe tonight, better to start it on a full stomach. The motel sat on Route 441, a rural two-lane running from the touristy strip in town all the way into the mountains to the north. Rather than a left, toward

SPEARFINGER

Kahleskawe's trailer, he took a right out of the parking lot and headed for town.

Barry the Prick

The sign out front said *Paul's* was a family restaurant with *the best burgers in town*. It sounded like just the thing: easy to eat in the car and would still be edible after hours on the passenger's seat. He hustled in and went straight to the hostess stand, with its attending twenty-something and her bright smile.

"How many in your party?"

"Just me, and it's to go. Can I—" He grabbed a menu from the pocket on the side of the stand.

"Well, sure, just help yourself."

He gave it a quick scan, noting both the buffalo burgers (*Have they never heard of cows?*) and chicken tenders (*Probably better as leftovers.*), ordered both, along with two large coffees, and handed over his debit card.

His name rang out from the hubbub in the restaurant behind him. "Spaberg? What the hell are *you* doing here?"

His muscles tensed, weight balancing on the balls of his feet, reflexes screaming to turn and face the threat—that oh-so-familiar voice—but his will clamped down like a thing of iron. The nape of his neck crawling, he accepted his card from the hostess, signed the slip with a flourish, and took his time returning the card to his wallet and the wallet to his pocket before turning with every ounce of casualness he was able to summon. He scanned the dining area, then obviously—and needlessly—scanned it again, before squinting in feigned surprise.

"Barry? Barry, uh, *Stone*, isn't it?"

Barry Stone sat sharing a table with Abby Haines, her twenty-something camera guy, and his own wide grin.

"Nice try, *Spaz*-berg, but I know you know me."

Ignoring Barry (though a more physically inclined man might have been tempted to punch him right in that smarmy smile), Carl walked to the table, holding out a hand to Abby. "Carl Spaberg. Nice to meet you."

Abby was dark haired, dark eyed, and pretty, though without the glossy, pampered look so common among talking heads and news anchors. And smart—too smart by half, from what he'd seen of her stand-ups and field reporting, to settle for being a mere *news presenter*. She wasn't working in print, but Carl had a lot more respect for the TV folks who actually came out into the field, writing their own headlines and stories, often putting their reports together on the fly, trying to be the first to get in front of a camera and break their news to the world. It was a bit slap-dash, lacking the majesty of working for a major paper, the precision of crafting and then retooling the words to create the perfect story, but it was a skill nonetheless. Call it a lesser skill, like comparing the speed chess played by old men in the park to the game of kings exhibited by the grandmasters in world class matches that were studied around the globe.

"Connor Day." The cameraman thrust out his own hand. "You in the industry?"

"I—"

"Are you kidding?" Barry crowed. "My man Carl, here, is on the reporting fast track! Of course, he's heading down while the rest of us are going up, but hey, less traffic in that direction, right Carl?"

"Nice to meet you," Abby finally responded, though her gaze was dismissive and she showed no surprise at Barry's words.

She's heard of me.

Though fame was something Carl sought every day—had for his entire reporting career—being *infamous* was a different thing entirely, something he'd quickly found not to his liking. He started wishing he'd not ordered his burger well-done; it'd take longer that way, and he just wanted to get the hell out of there.

Moving on auto-pilot, Carl had taken Connor's proffered hand, and was still shaking it as the young man glanced from Carl to Barry before finally settling on Abby, sudden crow's feet showing his confusion. "I'm sorry, am I missing something here?"

Barry's eyes gleamed. "You mean you don't *know*? Oh, I—"

"I'm a print reporter," Carl said, indicating Barry. "Like him, I—"

"Carl? Let me tell it." It wasn't a request, and Barry practically shouted in his excitement. Abby looked a little embarrassed at the commotion, as if she wished: A) Carl had never come into Paul's, B) that she'd never sat with Barry, or C) both. It was probably C. "I know you're tired of the story, but *man*, I gotta say, this shit *never* gets old for me."

He faced Connor. "See, my man here was working for the *Eagle-Tribune*, a paper in Boston. It's not *The Globe* or anything, but it's respectable enough, and he's on his way up. At least, that's what he's telling anybody who'll listen. He'll be on the cover of *Time* soon, win a Pulitzer, shit like that. Anyway, dude comes into the office hawking a story about something he saw while on a trip up in Maine. None of the other papers in town will touch it. But Carl, here, he touches it. He takes it and runs with it, drives up to Maine for some of his Pulitzer-worthy investigative journalism, and actually comes back with a story."

"Yeah?" Connor looked impressed, but Carl's heart was in his shoes; he knew what was coming.

"Yeah." Barry positively glowed, raising his hands to frame an imaginary headline. "'Monsters in Maine!'"

Connor blinked. "Huh?"

If Barry's grin grew any wider, the top of his head would fall off—an image Carl found somewhat comforting. "That's what his editor at the *Eagle-Tribune* said, but Carl was all 'You're gonna print this story or I'll take it somewhere else,' and his editor was all 'Have at it, dude, take it on down the road.' So he did."

Barry leaned back a few degrees, giving Carl a look he probably thought of as *appraising*. The tit.

"I have to admit, my man here stuck to his guns. Way more than I would have. He went from paper to paper, trying to freelance the story—"

"Because I believe in the work," Carl said. "And I'm damned good at it. And it was a good st—"

"He finally wound up at *The Weekly World Mirror*."

"Wait," said Connor. "You mean that comic book thing at the supermarket checkout? The one with headlines about suburban Bigfoot and that rat girl?"

Barry managed to grin wider without the top of his skull popping loose. Carl was disappointed.

"That's the one. Carl strolled into their offices last year, monster story in hand . . . and that's where he stayed."

His grin was huge, his voice gleeful. "I mean, you're still there, right Carl? You're down here on their dime?"

"But they're not—" Connor looked at Carl, blushing over what had nearly slipped from his mouth. Barry, however, had no qualms.

"Not a real paper, you mean? Nope." He looked at Carl then glanced at Abby to see if she was paying attention while he schooled the tabloider. To her credit, it didn't appear she was enjoying Barry at all anymore. "Not the kind of place people win Pulitzers from."

Carl was seething. It took everything he had not to let it show. He took a breath. Let it out. "Barry, I wish I could be there to see your face."

"Where? When?"

The swinging kitchen doors opened and closed with a *fluff-fluff*, emitting a puff of onion-and-garlic-scented air along with the hostess bearing a paper bag.

"Your to-go order's ready, sir!"

Carl glanced at her, then focused on Barry again.

"Wherever you are when I go flying by and leave you eating my dust. Nice meeting you, Connor. Abby. My condolences on the company you keep."

He turned before Barry could respond, thanked the hostess, took his bag, and stalked out the door. He was still seething, wishing he'd come up with a better exit line, something sharper, pithier. He stepped off the sidewalk on the way to his rental. Stopped. Took a step back. Looked to his left, at the dashboard of the Toyota Corolla beside him.

There sat a press ID, with Barry the prick's picture on it.

"Oh, you have got to be shitting me."

He thought about his parting shot to Barry and felt himself breaking out in a slightly manic grin. He was still grinning as he opened his own passenger's side door, put the food bag on the seat, and opened the glove box to rummage for the small tool kit he always traveled with.

His grin had only grown when, five minutes later, he pulled out of the lot, turning north, toward Kahleskawe's trailer. Somewhere up the road, he'd toss out the stem caps rattling in the ashtray, as well as the shiny bits of metal from the center of the Corolla's valve stems, neatly unscrewed with his needle-nose pliers. He thought of Barry's face when he came out of Paul's to find his car sitting six inches lower than when he'd gone in, all four tires completely undamaged but unable to hold an ounce of air until those valve cores had been replaced.

Carl giggled as he motored away, leaving Barry to eat his dust.

On Stakeout: One

"Shit. This might be harder than I thought."

Thomas Kahleskawe's trailer sat beneath the red maple on its low rise, in the middle of a clearing just off a tertiary highway. His was the only dwelling in sight, and his dirt driveway seemed the only 'road' around besides the ribbon of two-lane blacktop Carl had rolled to a stop on. In Boston, Somerville, Cambridge, Brookline—you know, fucking *civilization*—there was always something to hide behind. A few cars to park between, a building to lean against, a doorway to hang out in. Whatever you were watching, there was likely a Starbucks within a stone's throw with a front window you could sit in, nursing coffees and muffins while keeping an eye on your subject—and if not a Starbucks, there was *definitely* a Dunks.

Out here, there was none of that. There was practically nothing at all.

What am I going to do? Park behind a tree or something?

Even if he left the sedan up on the road and slipped into the woods at the edge of Kahleskawe's clearing, if Tuckwa showed up to visit his great-grandfather, Carl's car would be sitting in plain sight.

How the fuck do people live *like this? Seriously, I haven't been this far out in the boonies since—*

Since he'd driven up to Maine, following the story that'd gotten him where he was today. *Aw, shit.* He glanced around at the trees. *I've got a bad feeling about this.*

He got a grip on himself and did the only thing he could think of: he drove a quarter mile down the road and pulled off, across the shoulder and into the trees, trying to aim for level, solid-looking ground. The rental didn't have four-wheel drive, and he didn't relish the thought of having to call for a tow; his newsy brethren back in town were sure to get wind that he'd driven all the way out there, only to get stuck in the mud.

He was just throwing the gearshift into park when his phone rang; the caller ID read *Cherokee Police*.

"Hello?"

"Carl Spaberg?"

"Officer Nelawe? So good to hear from you. I—"

"Please hold for Chief Tuckwa."

Muzak, actual elevator music from the 70s. He just had time to think *Still running from my charms, I see* before, with a *click*, Charlie Tuckwa's flat voice was in his ear.

"Spaberg? Where are you? We stopped by your room, but you're not there."

Carl gazed through his windshield, at the trees, trees, and more trees. "Just taking in the local sights, Chief. It's not like I get out this way very *ever*, so—"

"Listen, Carl, you've heard about the press conference tomorrow?"

So, he was *Carl* now? He was instantly on guard. The shift to a first-name basis meant one of two things: In an interview room, it was a passive form of intimidation, *Officer This* and *Sergeant That* interviewing *Jim* or *Tom*, like adults talking down to a child. But they weren't in an interview room, so Tuckwa was actually trying to appear friendly.

Which means he wants something. "Yeeessss . . .?"

"We've been discussing things here in my office, and—"

"Who's we?"

"Well, it's my office, and I'm Chief of Police, so it's pretty safe to assume we're cops. We've been talking over the Kanoska/Ghigooie case, and someone suggested . . . well, we'd like to ask you a favor."

I knew it!

"We've got something we'd like to hold back, you know, something to not put in the papers to help weed out the crackpots. Have you told anyone about the, uh, the organ harvesting?"

"From the kids? No, I haven't."

"We'd like you not to."

"*We* being you and the feds."

"Yes. Someone here made the suggestion, and I think it's a good one. They also suggested I make a plea to your humanity, to point out that it would really benefit the investigation and help keep any panic down."

"Yeah?"

"Yeah. But I've met you, so instead I'll point out how keeping quiet could be beneficial to you, personally."

"I'm touched."

"Yeah. Look, *The Weekly World Mirror* is just that: a weekly. There are going to be daily papers there tomorrow. TV people, too. Right now, you've got what you guys call *a scoop*, am I right?"

"Some might call it that."

"They put it all over their headlines and in the news scrawl tomorrow, then they break that story and you lose your edge, right?"

Though the print copy was an old-fashioned weekly—something Carl privately appreciated—this was the information age. Smaller stories went up on the *Mirror*'s website almost every day, and there were a couple of blog-style daily columns. If he *had* to, Carl could break a story in about a half an hour, whenever he wanted.

But there was no need for the chief to know that. "You sure you don't have a journalism degree hidden in a drawer somewhere?"

"Bite your tongue. But you hold onto that until your paper comes out next week, that gives us a week to use it, and you still have your scoop on all the real papers."

"I like how you don't let your fierce regard for my feelings slow you down in any way from calling it like you see it."

"I'm good that way. So, will you agree not to write about the livers for a week? Just keep it to yourself?"

"Well, when you make your argument so suavely, what's a poor self-serving leech on the neck of society to do?"

"I . . . what? Is that a yes or a no?"

"It makes sense to me, Chief."

He disconnected the call and got out of the car. *Well*, he thought, hiking down the road toward Kahleskawe's driveway, binoculars bouncing on their neck strap, one hand full of a buffalo burger, the other clutching a still-hot cup of Joe. *That was . . . interesting. I honestly can't tell if he's up to something tricky, or if he's as straightlaced as he seems.*

I also don't know if this is really buffalo or if that's just a sales thing, but this is *a tasty burger!*

In the Tent

Nathan woke with a start, eyes opening to total blackness and definitely not in his own bed. But he felt the comforting pressure of Maggie's hip against his, smelled canvas, and at the sharp *zzzz* of the inner zipper, understood where he was and that at least one of the twins was crouching by his feet.

"What's going on?"

The sounds of someone fumbling with the tent flap ceased, and the following beat of silence actually *felt* guilty. Nate sat up on his elbows. He still couldn't see, but propping up like that just felt more authoritative. "Well?"

"I have to pee." The whisper was young and small, but definitely male.

Michael. "Well, just find a tree out at the edge of the site and be quick about—"

"Me, too." This whisper was even smaller, and from off beside Maggie.

Michelle, he thought, just as Maggie said, "Of course you do."

Well, now we're all up. "Okay, like I said, make it quick—*both of you*. Find a tree—not the same one—and—"

"And you can both take a little hike down to the bath house," said Maggie, "and go there."

"Aw, Mom," Michael whined. "I don't wanna go to the bath house." His tone shifted to excited. "I wanna pee on a tree."

"*I* don't want to pee on a tree." There was a nylon-on-nylon *swish-swish* as Michelle wormed out of her sleeping bag. "Yuck!"

"You're not," said Maggie. "Put your sneakers on and make sure you grab a flashlight."

"Well, *I'm* peeing on a tree," Michael announced, unzipping the other tent flap.

"*You* are walking your nine-year-old sister down to the bath house, like a good brother should," said Maggie.

"I'm nine too!"

"Hon," Nathan said. "The bath house is down at the end of the road. It's like a four-or-five-minute walk. Why don't they just each pick a tree and—"

"Because I don't want my little girl accidentally squatting in some poison ivy in the dark. I knew a girl who did that once, back in junior high, and it was *awful.*"

Nathan Messing came from a camping family; Maggie did not. After waxing practically poetic about canoeing and fishing with his mom and dad when he was a kid, Nathan had finally sold them on a family camping trip. As a bona-fide girly-girl, Maggie had nearly called the whole thing off when he'd proposed a tent rather than renting a cabin with its own hot and cold running water and a solid door she could close between herself and the actual *wilderness.*

He'd calmed her—mostly—with some brochure pictures of the bath house: public, yes, but sparkling clean (at least in the promo material) with hot and cold running water and—best of all, as far as Maggie was concerned—showers. When they'd arrived that morning after a two-hour drive in their packed-to-the-gills Durango, he'd had to talk her out of the site closest to the bath house.

It's like being seated at a restaurant, he'd pointed out. *Do you really want to hear it every time anyone flushes the toilet?*

Now, though, he was kind of wishing he'd gone with her suggestion. "It's pretty dark out there. One of us should go with them." He worked down his sleeping bag's zipper. Maggie wasn't at her best when woken from a sound sleep, and rather than argue about it, he'd just man up.

Michael said, "Aw, Dad, it's just the end of the road! And we'll have a flashlight! We can do it on our own!"

Ten seconds ago, he didn't want to go at all, Nate thought. *I guess the only thing worse than having to escort his sister somewhere is having his dad tag along. Still, it's dark, and they're only nine years—*

Maggie's hand slipped into the freshly opened sleeping bag, skimmed up his thigh and into the loose leg of his boxers, found his cock, and gave it a friendly squeeze. He barely managed not to yelp at her first unexpected touch; the squeeze brought a quiet gasp.

"It's only a *ten- or twelve-minute round trip,*" she said, emphasizing the last six words with little pulses of pressure that had an immediate effect. "I think they'll be fine, don't you?"

Ten or twelve minutes? he thought. *Plenty of time!*

Back in their childless days, they both would have laughed at the thought that ten minutes could be *enough* time, never mind *plenty*. But as the still-young parents of a pair of intelligent and active twins for the past nine years, they'd had to learn different—sometimes sneakier, ofttimes speedier—ways of getting the job done. The fact that Maggie was already in the mood was half the battle—more—where married life speed-sex was concerned.

"Uh . . ." he said, rather stupidly.

69

Inside his shorts, Maggie's thumb slipped back and forth across the sensitive spot just under the head of his cock as she asked again, so close her breath tickled his ear: "Don't you?"

"Zip the tent closed behind you to keep the bugs out," he nearly shouted. Some still-rational part of him understood the zipper would both slow the kids down and act as a last-minute warning of their return if ten minutes *wasn't* long enough—though the way Maggie's breathing sounded against his neck as her hand worked, he *really* didn't think that would be a problem.

They remained still—well, mostly—while the kids slipped into their sneakers and found the flashlight Nate had set by the tentrance, but once they were on the other side of the canvas, Maggie was on the move. "I don't know whether it's all the fresh air or what," she breathed into his ear as the kids re-zipped the tent. Nate didn't know either, and he sure didn't care as his wife slipped from her bag into his, her own sleeping shorts somehow having vanished in the night. As the twins' voices moved out toward the road, arguing over who would hold the flashlight, he spent a single moment wondering if letting two nine-year-olds head out to the bath house alone was really all that smart. Then, the little head took over and he stopped thinking—a relinquishing of control he'd live to regret, if only briefly.

Ten minutes would be plenty of time.

Michelle and Michael

Michelle zipped the tent as Michael found the dirt road leading to the bath house, slashing the flashlight beam from tree to tree and making his "Zzzzzm, zzzzzm-zzzm" lightsaber sounds. Mom's quiet giggle rose into the night as Michelle turned to follow, and the little girl rolled her eyes.

They're probably gonna be doing sex while we're gone.

She wasn't quite sure what sex was, but she knew her mom and dad did it. Her best friend Tanya's big sister, Sheri, said so, and she was thirteen and knew all kinds of stuff. Michelle figured it was gross, and had something to do with the way Mom and Dad kissed sometimes: not the dry, puckery, *mmmwa* way they kissed her and Michael, but more like they were trying to eat each other's faces. She couldn't figure out why Mom and Dad could do that, but Mom freaked out when Tanya and Michelle took turns chewing the same piece of gum. It made *no* sense.

Lots of things parents did didn't make sense. She was pretty sure that was kind of what made them parents.

She caught up to Michael as he did a jump-spin-slash she was positive would have taken his leg off had that been a *real* lightsaber. "Let me hold the flashlight."

"Nope." He took another couple of swings, then made the *turning off the lightsaber* noise, though he didn't turn off the light. "Zzzzzm, zzzzzzm. Zzzzzup! Mom told me to take you to the bathroom, so I'm taking you. That means I get the light."

"Nu-uh! She said to *walk* me there."

"Same thing."

"Nuh-uh! I'll hold it there; you hold it back."

"Nope. I'm walking you, and I'm older."

"Wow, eight whole minutes."

Her brother's voice took on a teasing lilt. "I *could* just turn it off . . ."

With a quiet *click*, the bright beam disappeared, plunging them into darkness. Normally, Michelle didn't have a problem with the dark. But this was, like, *dark*-dark, and it unnerved her that Michael could put an end to it while she could not. This wasn't home, where she knew what was around and where everything was: there were bushes, and trees, and more trees, and once she couldn't see any of it, Michelle had the instant impression it was all looking at her, watching her somehow from the darker shadows.

"Quit it!"

"Sure." The light reappeared, showing her a grinning Michael and, dimly, the first rank of trees about them. Whatever loomed behind those was still hidden, but that she could see at all was a comfort.

"So, I get to keep the light?"

She could see from his smirk he considered it settled. He knew he'd scared her. She thought about calling for Mom, telling her Michael was being a butt munch, but she remembered that giggle. *If they're doing sex*, she thought, *I'll probably get yelled at for bugging them.*

She wondered for a moment if Michael knew what was going on in the tent, but rejected the idea. She thought he might know about sex, but not as much as her. Sheri wasn't telling *him* stuff all the time, and besides, he might be eight minutes older, but girls matured faster than boys. She wasn't *exactly* clear on what that meant either, but Sheri said it, so it must be so.

"Lead the way, butt munch." He'd won this round, but she'd have her revenge. Besides, she *really* had to pee.

"I know you are, but what am I?" He started down the road and she followed, sticking close to that light.

"A butt munch."

"I know you are, but what am I?"

On Stakeout: Two

Carl found a halfway comfortable spot in the trees near the end of Kahleskawe's driveway, with a good view of the front of the trailer and its—so far as he knew—only door. He sipped his coffee—also pretty decent, maybe there was hope for this wilderness-riddled hellhole yet—and trained his binoculars on the squat lump with the satellite dish. He immediately noticed the lack of any vehicle, but thinking back, there hadn't been one the last time he'd been there either.

Maybe he doesn't drive, he thought. *What's he, about a thousand years old? Be the responsible thing to do, turn in your license when you hit around seven hundred or so.*

But with no vehicle to use as a tell, there was no way to be sure the old man was actually home. He briefly considered sneaking up to a window, but chucked the idea.

Way too much open ground to cover. Sneak or sprint, he'll have so much time to see me, I may as well just knock and see if he answers the door. Man, I hate it out here in the sticks.

He watched for a couple of hours, interspersed with a few solo games of Word With Friends when he just couldn't stand the boredom. When dusk fell, he had the joy of seeing one of the front windows remain lit from within—silvery, flickering light he immediately associated with a wall-sized flatscreen TV. It didn't necessarily mean anyone was actually in there watching it, but he thought the odds were in his favor.

Following the dusk, however, came the night, winnowing its way between the trees; darkness so thick he felt it crowding him. There were no streetlights, and no sign of the lights of town. The sky above was filled with more stars than he'd ever seen in his life, but Carl Spaberg was a city boy, born and raised, and right then if it wasn't a bright, steady electric light, he wasn't interested. He watched that single flickering window, hyper-aware he was lurking outside the home of someone he suspected of being a serial killer, and though by daylight Kahleskawe had seemed slow and frail, in the inky night outside his trailer, Carl recalled only that the killing knife had been razor sharp.

And never mind all that, it was nighttime in the woods! Carl made the mistake of Googling *wild predators of North Carolina* on his phone and had 34,200,000 results in 0.76 seconds. He opened the first link and scanned the list.

The black bear? Bobcat? Coyote? Feral swine? He paused at that one. *Swine? They have man-eating pigs in this shithole? Christ, that's right out of a fucking horror movie! Nutrias, red foxes, red wolves—Wait! They have* nutrias? *I don't even know what that is, but I know I don't like the sound of it. This is bullshit, I'm gonna—What was that?*

He froze, listening to the shadows move about him under the trees. He could have sworn he'd heard a twig snap. Or maybe it was a grunt. Yeah, it definitely *could* have been a grunt, or maybe a growl—unless, of course, it had been leaves rustling as a large heavy body brushed through them. Like a bobcat. Or a bear. Or maybe a fucking *nutria*. Or—

There it was again! Maybe.

And he had the impression that whatever it was had gotten closer. If he'd heard it. Which he most certainly almost had. It was—

"Fuck this." He fled the shadows of the forest for the dim safety of the road—then discovered, once out there in the relative open, he couldn't see into the shadows beneath the trees to either side of the tarmac.

Shit.

He hustled toward the car, swinging his phone's light this way and that. He had a moment of concern (really more like five minutes of nearly pants-shitting panic) when he couldn't find it, but his light finally glinted off something under the trees, and he fell into the driver's seat with a sense of relief bordering on the orgasmic.

He pounded down that second cup of coffee cold, hoping the jolt of caffeine would help calm his nerves, then drove back to Kahleskawe's driveway *sans* lights. He passed it twice in the dark, but finally parked again, the sedan hopefully screened from the trailer's view by trees while Carl could at least see the lighted window. He locked the doors and settled in to keep an eye on that light.

I'll just move the car at dawn, before he has a chance to see me, he thought. But comfortably surrounded by steel and glass, worn out in the wake of his panic adrenaline, it wasn't an hour before he felt drowsy. His head nodded and he snapped awake. He sat straighter, blew a few deep breaths, and cracked his knuckles. He ran through what he had, both as a theory (the long list) and actual proof (what list?), trying to keep his mind active, but it wasn't long before he nodded again. He jerked awake and straightened, but slower this time. He just had time to think *Is that thunder?* and look up through the windshield at the endless stars showing in the cloudless night sky before he was asleep.

Nate and Maggie

Ten minutes had been *more* than enough time, for both of them. In fact, Nate had been tempted to try again—*was* there something about the mountain air?—but his twenties were far behind him, and he hadn't been able to be ready again *that* fast since his teens. Besides, orgasms tended to make him sleepy, and though the ground was far from comfortable (he'd forgotten about *that* part of camping, apparently) his sleeping bag was warm, and he had his pillow, and—

Something jabbed into his ribs, a quick one-two-three, jerking him back from the precipice of sleep nearly hard enough to give him whiplash.

Maggie's finger.

"Hey, what about the kids?"

"Mrphle?" Nate blinked, but in the pitch black inside their tent, opening or closing his eyes made no difference.

"The kids? Remember them?"

The finger jabbed again. Nate scooted away. "I'm up! I'm up! Jesus . . . What, you think the kids saw us?"

"No! It's—haven't they been gone too long?"

"Well . . . we said ten or twelve minutes, right?"

"It's been more than fifteen." Her voice was full of concern. "Maybe closer to twenty."

He didn't argue or offer his own estimate; they'd known for almost a decade and a half Maggie had a far better time sense than he. He rubbed a hand over his face, pressing on his closed eyelids until bright colors swirled in a phantom vision, trying to squeeze the last of the sleep from them.

"What if they got lost?"

"It's a straight road. And they know what our car looks like. As long as they had a flashlight—"

"They're only nine, and it's really dark out there."

Trying very hard not to point out that was what *he'd* said, he rolled onto his side in his *very* warm and cozy sleeping bag, feeling it when they made eye contact though neither of them could actually see.

"Well, one of us should go out and find them, then, don't you think?"

Michelle

Michelle washed her hands thoroughly, then used paper towels to dry every last millimeter of skin. Michael had already been calling her awhile, and she pictured him standing outside, alone in that mondo-spooky crossroads where the bath house sat. A streetlight illuminated the low wooden building with MEN's and WOMEN's doors at either end and a camp bulletin board in the middle, and they'd been able to see that light the whole time as they'd made their way there. Honestly, Michelle hadn't thought they even needed the flashlight: the lane was so straight, it had been simple to just head toward the light.

But they'd come out of their road to find that, from the bathhouse, three *other* roads lead away toward other parts of the campground. They'd seen all three earlier. They'd known the roads were there. But looking down them now was different than when the sun had been in the sky: you could see as far as the streetlight fell and no farther, the oiled dirt pathways disappearing into black tree tunnels after just a few feet, like giant throats waiting to swallow up anyone foolish enough to venture in. She'd noticed how frightening those three were and had congratulated herself on not having to go down something as dark and weird as that ... until she'd turned to look down the road they'd just emerged from and found it was the darkest and weirdest of all.

She imagined Michael waiting for her, alone, looking down one road after another, shining his light and trying to see farther along each throat. Michael was an imaginative boy—Mom said that, and Michelle knew what it meant—and she knew from trying it as they'd stood out front arguing over the flashlight again (the longer they'd bickered, the longer it put off separating, each actually being alone in this creepy place), that whenever you were looking down one dark and hungry throat, there was another at your back. She didn't know if Michael had felt like things out in the dark were watching them from behind no matter which way they'd faced, but she had.

He was an imaginative boy; if he were out there long enough, it *would* occur to him.

She smiled and washed her hands again.

Michael called her name just as she finished rinsing. He'd moved from the street closer to the door, though she knew he'd never come *in* the ladies' room. He also sounded nervous, which widened her smile.

Serves you right for being such a butt munch.

Thunder rumbled as she shut the water off, returned to the paper towel dispenser, and started drying.

"C'mon, Michelle!" He was just outside the open doorway. "It's gonna rain. Quit playing in the toilet with the rest of the turds, or whatever you're doing. Mom'll be mad if we come back all soaked."

But Mom wasn't there right then, and Michael sounded *really* spooked. Michelle grinned as she made *very* sure the spaces between her fingers were dry.

"Mom?" Michael said. "It's not my fault. Michelle won't come out of the bathroom."

Not falling for it, she thought. *Nice try, though*.

And it was. Michael even sounded relieved rather than scared. But he'd done that before, pretended to be telling on her when Mom wasn't really there, and—

And a voice answered him. It was too quiet and far from the door for her to make out the actual words, but it was definitely *not* Michael.

Oh my God!

Michael said something else but she barely heard it over the *clatter-bang* as she shoved her paper towels into the trash can. She hurried to the door, marshalling her *you always tell me to wash my hands* argument and *Michael wouldn't share the flashlight* tactic. She stepped through the door already chirping "Hi, Mom," in her cheerfullest voice.

Michael lay in the dirt under the bulletin board, Mom squatting over him, still wearing her sleep shorts and oversized T-shirt, tickling his sides and tummy. Michelle's first thought, *If she's tickling him, we* can't *be in trouble!* was followed by confusion. Michael was *super* ticklish—just another area where non-ticklish Michelle was *clearly* superior—but he wasn't giggling or squirming, which *always* happened whenever Mom or Dad dropped the tickle-hammer on him. He just lay in the dirt, not even looking at Mom but staring instead at Michelle, eyes wide, as Mom gouged and dug at his side.

Well, maybe Mom was doing a bad job, like when kids at school didn't believe Michelle wasn't ticklish so they just tickled harder, until it hurt, then claimed victory when she squirmed and asked them to stop. But Michael wasn't squirming, and Mom was poking at his ribs so hard he flopped and rolled. He flopped and rolled so hard something looked wrong with his neck. And why was he staring like that? His eyes looked funny, and it was creepy, and he wasn't saying anything, but if there really *was* something wrong—

Michael lurched as Mom gave an extra-hard shove, and there was a sharp *crack*. Something splatted right into the middle of the bulletin board, thick and red, reminding Michelle of when some boy had stomped on cafeteria ketchup packets in the schoolyard, popping them like zits, squirting streaks of red across the ground—streaks just like up there on the board. But why would Mom have ketchup? And what was wrong with Michael? There was only one person there to ask, really, but this whole thing was weird, and Michelle felt afraid though she wasn't exactly sure why.

"Mom . . . ?"

Mom turned to look up at her. Her blonde hair was tousled, her clothes disheveled, like she'd just woken up. It's what Mom looked like every morning until she'd had her first cup of coffee—except for her eyes, which were normally kind of squinty right after waking but right now were wide open and alert.

Well, those and the beard of blood ringing her mouth.

Her turn had let more of Michael into view, including the way his own T-shirt was rucked up to show a thing on his side, a moist thing, all gooshy and gross, like last Thanksgiving, when the fat squirrel from across the street had finally gotten their Halloween pumpkins—not the Jack-O-Lanterns, but the whole pumpkins—gnawing holes into their sides to scoop out pawfulls of seeds and their accompanying goop. Only *this* gooshy gross hole wasn't orange but red, and bigger than a squirrel hole, even a fat one. And Mom hadn't scooped out a pawful of seeds but a *thing*, all purple and meaty. Even as

84

she gazed up at her daughter, she lifted it to her glistening lips and took another bite; it made a wet, cloth-tearing sound that caused Michelle's recently-emptied bladder to squirt just a little more pee.

"*Mom?*"

Mom chewed, and even at nine Michelle knew why her brother flopped and rolled so bonelessly. None of this made sense, none of it at all, but Michael was—

He's dead and she's eating him, like on The Walking Dead, *but she's not a zombie. She's not.*

And she wasn't. Michelle had seen *The Walking Dead*—she and Tanya watching on Sheri's phone, of course—and she knew that even with the freshest, newest ones, their eyes were always dead and cold. All you had to do was look.

But Mom's eyes seemed normal, gazing *at* Michelle, not blankly *through* her, and though she was terrified by what had happened to Michael, by what her mother was doing, Michelle was also confused: she wanted to be held and comforted and told everything would be okay, but the one who always did that was—

"Mommy?"

Mommy gulped down the last of the meaty red thing, and her eyes, which had been gazing at Michelle since she'd looked up, suddenly changed: their focus sharpened; they looked *hungry*. And her lips, outlined in a thick, gory clown smile, split in a hideous grin.

"*No.*"

Nathan

Nate trudged, his sneakers' untied laces flicking about in his flashlight's beam as he passed the last of the sites on the road; only another ten yards or so before he reached the crossroads that had been the twins' destination.

"The sex wasn't my idea," he muttered. "Sending the kids to the bath house wasn't my idea. Hell, I was against sending them alone in the *first* place! So why do *I* have to go bring them back?"

He knew why. Because though the sex hadn't been his idea, it had been, well . . . it had been hot as *hell* was what it had been! Fast and urgent and just . . . fucking wow. If he wanted that again—and hell *yeah* he did—he'd better keep Maggie happy. And up here in the mountain air. Or surrounded by trees. Or in the tent. Shit, he didn't know *what* it was, but he wanted to take advantage of it while it lasted, so . . . so he was the one to get out of his warm, snug sleeping bag, put on pants and sneakers, and head up the road in search of the probably bickering twins.

Besides, once Maggie'd pointed out how long they'd been gone, all Nate's pre-boning concerns had flooded back; even if Maggie *had* gone out to fetch the kids, he would have gone with her rather than simply lie there waiting. He—

A small scream cut the night, high and thin and brief—so brief, anyone else might have thought it the yip of a dog, maybe some nightbird—but Nate recognized the voice, receiving the signal just as nature had intended when it had created the maternal/paternal instinct.

"Michelle!"

He was sprinting before his own cry was finished, flashlight swinging as his arms pumped, eyes fixed only on the lighted crossroad ahead. He stumbled, stepped on some *whatever* that rolled, and almost went down, but caught himself. His right sneaker slipped half off in the stutter-step, but there was no time to stop; with his next stride it flew off into the night. It had been twenty years since high school track, but he took the turn toward the public bathrooms like he was rounding the bend in the 440, arms and legs working together, though his breathing was ragged, head filled with images garnered from decades of news footage and horror movies as he burst from the dark.

Michael lay on the ground, small and pale under the sodium vapor light, his clothing yanked askew and something wrong—oh, God, *so* wrong—with his side. Nate started to swerve toward him, but a sound came from the open ladies' room, the hard *whap* of a stall door slamming open, and his mind nearly cracked mid stride: two kids, two places, one Dad, what the *fuck* was he going to *do*?

Then, on the heels of the *whap* came a less-identifiable *thud*, and priorities fell into place in his head: something had happened to Michael, but something was *still happening* to Michelle, and whatever it was he could stop it, he *would* stop it—and kill whoever was doing it. Kill them fucking dead.

And approaching-middle-age Nathan Messing, without a plan, without a weapon, hell, without having even been in a fight since the third grade, never even thought of calling for help, but raced past his broken son (*can't look at him I'll stop if I look at him*) and burst into the ladies' restroom, fully intending to murder the motherfucker who was hurting his kids.

There were a half dozen toilet stalls, but only the one on the end—the closest—had someone's backside sticking out the open door. The backside, clad in a pair of shorts, jostled about as its owner worked on something deeper within the stall. Nate moved to plant his toe right in the center of those shorts, right in the fucking *taint* if he could find it, planning to start stomping this sick fuck's ass by first kicking it up around his ears as a kind of *attention getter*—

But it was a *woman's* ass.

In all the news coverage that had left a serious, lasting mark on him, all the movies and books that had formed his general *sick fuck* preconception, the sick fuck had been male. Retarded socially, stunted emotionally, abused as a child himself maybe, but almost always *male*. The women in the stories were most often some kind of caregiver, either medically or emotionally, and though these concepts were flying through his head *as* concepts rather than slowing down into anything even approaching words, they were enough to jam him up. He stuttered to a stop, mentally shifting from *seek and destroy* to—

"What's going on?"

The shorts shifted back, the woman straightened, turned, and Nate's eyes widened.

"Maggie? What are—"

His brain shifted again, dropping into straight-up neutral, bits of his mental make-up whirring along at tremendous speed, but none of those parts touching any other parts, a redlining motor with zero traction.

He'd left Maggie still in her sleeping bag when he'd zipped the tent closed, waved goodbye to her as he'd shut her inside, yet here she was, somehow already here and handling things. But what about Michael, lying outside, hurt bad—maybe *dead*—but here Maggie was, doing *whatever* in the ladies' room. Helping Michelle? Where was she? And what was smeared all about Maggie's mouth, a mouth he'd been kissing just ten minutes earlier? And all over her T-shirt? And on the stall wall he could see, that thin looping line with more spattered about it?

And as Maggie continued to turn toward him—everything moving oh-so-slowly as the needle on his speeding, tractionless mind passed through the red zone and hit the pin, maxed out but somehow still going faster, straining toward a blown gasket, a warped head, a *seriously explosive failure*—he saw beyond her, saw what she'd been working on as he'd burst into the scene; his little girl, tiny and beautiful, perched not on the toilet seat but up on the plumbing above the bowl, like she'd been hiding in the stall, feet tucked up so as not to show. Her own shirt hadn't been shoved up like Michael's, but torn open, her shoulders twisted and shoved toward the corner, exposing the wound in her side, the hole in his baby. But unlike Michael's, Nate *saw* this. Couldn't look *away* from this. Couldn't look away from the fist-sized tear in his baby's flesh, from the hole—Christ, so deep it might have gone *through* her—the pink ends of ribs poking out like the stove-in slats of an old crate. Couldn't look away from the blood splattering up the stall walls, so fresh it still collected and ran in thin rivulets toward the floor. Couldn't look away from her little face, the right side pressed tight to the wall, the left so perfect, untouched by all the trauma except for the look in the eye, so expressive, showing confusion and horror and pain and—

And it blinked.

She's alive!

The shifter in Nate's head slammed into gear, popping the clutch like it was trying to fire his speeding brain right out his ass. He lurched into motion, not really seeing Maggie, registering her only as something he had to get by to get to his little girl, who was *alive*, who *needed* him! His blood-caked wife came around, her right hand swinging at him in a fast backhand, something long and sharp *wicking* through the air as Nate vaulted forward like a sprinter leaving the blocks, going from a standstill to a full sprint in the space of a single step—a step which left his bare right foot slipping in the blood he'd not noticed slicking the floor.

Nate never even saw the blade as he dove inside Maggie's reach, but her forearm struck his shoulder like a bat wielded by a giant. His humorous snapped, his feet left the tiles, and he was launched across the bathroom. One of his left ribs snapped against the sink; that pain met the agony from his shattered right arm in the middle, neatly pinching off his shriek, and he flopped to the floor unable to breathe, crawl, or see his daughter anymore. He rolled onto his back—*that* part of him didn't hurt, not yet—and she was coming.

Maggie followed him across the bath house, and Nate wondered if he'd hit his head, too, because the whole building seemed to shudder, the floor jolting in time with her feet. He saw the blade in her right hand, like a straight razor a foot long and shiny black.

"Maggie?" He sucked a shallow breath. It was all he could manage. "What are you doing?" He nearly pointed, but opted to keep his good arm pressed to the agony that now lived in his left side. "What about . . ." Another breath. ". . . Michelle?"

He pushed with his feet, wanting to keep away from her while needing to get up and go to Michelle, but they merely paddled against the slick floor, slipping in his daughter's blood. Rather than answer, Maggie took a bite of something held in her left hand—Nate hadn't even noticed it, preoccupied with the huge knife—then tossed whatever it was into the sink above him. Fresh blood coated her chin, glistening in the fluorescents, as she silently grinned and leaned toward him.

"What the fuck!"

Maggie was surreal, but his daughter was dying mere feet away. He kicked into the exposed plumbing beneath the sink, planted his shod left foot against the heavy, industrial drain pipe, and *shoved*. His slickened back slid across the floor, away from the blood pooling beneath that last toilet stall and onto clean tiles. He aided the motion, cycling his feet with a breathy shrill, things that had once been joined in his side grinding together like a mortar and pestle milling a mixture of pain. He slowed as the fresh tiles wiped the slick from his back, but it *had* only been the first stall, and he hadn't far to go before his shoulders bumped against the low threshold at the open exit. The floor shuddered again, the rhythm of Maggie in casual pursuit as his head lolled, the back of his skull meeting nothing but air. Hanging back over the step down to the outside world, he saw an upside-down crossroads with its camp office just across the way, and an upside-down Maggie coming toward him from the darkened end of their road in her sleep shorts and oversized T-shirt, her feet shoved into tennis shoes, and—

Wait. What?

"Oh, my God!" upside-down Maggie cried. "Nate! *Michael*? Where's—"

It all came to him in a flash, making sudden sense of so many things that *hadn't* made sense.

Maggie didn't beat me here—that wasn't Maggie!

He'd seen Michelle blink; she might still be alive. Michael too—he'd run right past and not actually checked. He'd failed, but Maggie could go for help. Maggie could save them. Maggie could—

"*Run!*" He tried to scream, but all that emerged was a whispery whistle shaped like a word. She was still coming, running toward him. The *other* was still coming, too—he felt it in the floor. Though it hurt nearly as much as when the bones had broken, he pulled in an actual breath and reached up his good arm to grip the door frame.

Haven't done a single thing right tonight. Please, let me do this one thing. Please.

"Run!" he shouted—actually *shouted*, though something tore inside him—and yanked. He got one leg under him and pushed to his feet just as not-Maggie arrived. He flung himself forward, trying to bear her to the floor under his weight. He hadn't fought her well unharmed, and now he was *all* fucked up, but maybe he could tie her up, slow her down even if he lost consciousness, give the real Maggie a head start, a chance to get aw—

Not-Maggie stepped up practically chest-to-chest, but wasn't looking at Nate; she stared past him, out toward the street. Nate jolted to a stop as her right fist took him under the chin in an uppercut—though rather than following through, her fist merely held him there, the foot-long spike having punched up through his budding double chin, pierced both his tongue and the roof of his mouth, and slipped neatly between his right and left sinus cavities to thrust halfway through his brain.

SATURDAY

Thelma and Louise

"We got to go."

"Hrnh? Wzat?"

Carl opened bleary eyes. Saw a steering wheel. A dashboard. Beyond them lay a sunlit dirt drive leading through the trees to where, on a small rise, a lumpy trailer sat beneath a tree, a misshapen mole on the face of the land.

Fell asleep during a surveillance. Again.

He lifted his head, tried to straighten up, but a bolt of pain shot through his stiff neck, quashing any *get up and go* he might have been feeling. To be honest, there hadn't been a lot. It was all concentrated in his bladder now, which was *very* interested in his getting up and going. He recalled plans to move the car at dawn and closed his eyes, gently rolling his neck and shoulders, trying to loosen up a bit before reaching for the ignition.

Just in case he hasn't already seen me, I'll back up a few feet before I step out to take a leak. If I'm lucky, the old guy's a late riser, and—

"We have to go."

Carl tried to exit the vehicle like an Olympic runner leaving the blocks, but his left shoulder slammed into the door while his right thigh *thudded* the bottom of the steering wheel, and he couldn't be sure whether it was his skull bouncing off the window glass or the horrible grinding *twang* his completely un-loosened neck made as he cranked his gaze to the right that brought the tears to his eyes.

95

Thomas Kahleskawe sat in the passenger's seat, calmly regarding the flailing reporter.

"Holy *shit*fuck*fire*! What the *hell* are you doing here?" Carl checked the door locks. They were engaged. He clearly remembered locking the doors against the night, worried about North Carolina's ravaging wildlife. "How the hell did you get *in* here?"

"Does it matter?"

Despite his protesting neck, Carl scanned the interior of the car for any more surprises, glared at the obviously *useless* door locks, then focused on the old man again.

"Kinda, yeah!"

"The press conference is at nine o'clock. It is eight thirty now. We have to go."

"Eight thirty?" Carl checked his watch, dry-scrubbed his hands up and down his face a couple of times, then checked with his bladder: apparently, the sudden appearance of the old Cherokee had startled the need to piss right out of him. It'd be back—with a vengeance, he knew—but for now he was good to go. He looked at the old man. The subject of his surveillance had not only made him, but had hopped into his car like an ancient Thelma to Carl's Louise, looking for a ride into town.

Embarrassing if this got out, sure, but he was also sharing his car with his pick for *serial killer of the week*. He'd been thinking about it a lot, and maybe he was simply convincing himself, but the more he thought about it, the more possible-sliding-toward-probable it seemed, and waking up to find the man sitting there watching him sleep was surreal. He'd been jolted to alertness, and he had a metric ton of adrenaline pumping through his system, but Carl would be the first to admit he wasn't his sharpest until he'd had coffee. The caffeine deficit fogged things a bit, but he was slowly coming to grips with the situation.

If he'd wanted me dead, I'd be dead. Hell, I served myself up like some Peapod home murder service! So, if he is the killer, this had *to look suspicious. Why is he not wearing my head as a hat right now?*

A thought squirted from between his brain's slowly accelerating cogs, despite the lack of any dark roast, a way to fit it all into Carl's ongoing narrative.

He knows I'm a reporter—he must want *to talk, and he picked me! Like the Zodiac killer sending letters to Paul Avery!*

Well, he couldn't fault the old man's taste.

He scrabbled for questions. His first time interviewing a serial killer, he needed something clever, something punchy, something to ease himself into conversation with a madman—but his mental cogs weren't rolling *quite* up to speed yet, so he went with the first thing that had popped into his head.

"But seriously, how did you get in here?"

The old man made a disgusted *pah* at the question. "Are you going to the press conference?"

"Well . . . yeah."

"Not if you do not start the car." Kahleskawe faced forward, staring out the windshield and setting his shoulders, obviously considering the matter closed. Carl noticed that, while the other times he'd seen the old man Kahleskawe had been dressed sort of one-step-above-homeless casual, today he wore khakis and a white button-down shirt; a little incongruous, Carl thought, with his topknot.

Sunday-go-to-meeting clothes on a Saturday?

He reached for the keys, dangling in the ignition. "I take it you'd like a ride?"

"Why else would I be in your car?"

"Why, indeed?"

"I have things I must say to the chief of police."

"Uh-huh." Carl started the engine and gripped the shift lever, but paused. "You need to get to this meeting?"

"Yes."

"But you don't drive?"

"No."

Carl chewed on that a moment.

"What would you have done if I *hadn't* been here? Does this shitpoke town even *have* Uber?"

"What does it matter?" Kahleskawe stared ahead. "You are going there anyway, and I am already in your car."

The old face was expressionless, but something tickled Carl's internal antennae, and he grinned.

"You're doing the *muy mysterioso* thing on purpose, aren't you? You're deliberately winding me up!"

The world's oldest suspect remained stoic, silent and eyes-front as Carl started for town.

Well, Carl thought. *At least I have a captive interviewee.*

He scooped his phone from the dash and opened Google Maps, setting the Cherokee Cultural Arts Center as their destination and surreptitiously turning on his recorder. Rolling his shoulders and working his neck, still trying to get the kinks out, Carl just let his mouth off the leash a bit, asking questions as they occurred.

"You don't drive. So, you walk everywhere?"

Silence.

"What do you want to talk to the chief about?"

Silence.

"I only ask because, you know, you'll be speaking in front of a crowd. Maybe you want to throw your talking points back and forth a bit, sort of polish your delivery? I *am* rather famous for my facility with words. I don't want to pat myself on the back or anything, but . . ."

Kahleskawe's silence lasted about halfway to town, when the old man finally poked a stiffened finger toward the dashboard.

"That radio work?"

The Press Conference

They reached the Cultural Arts center with five minutes to spare. Carl tried to hustle in, but was held up by his passenger; however stealthy or magical the ex-didanawisgi had been getting *into* the car, he got *out* just like every other old man in the world: with grunts, groans, and the eventual, "Can you give me your hand?"

With a sigh, Carl hauled Kahleskawe—who looked like a bag of sticks, but was heavier than Carl'd expected—to his feet and again tried to hurry inside. His bladder had recovered, and if he didn't get in there at least a couple of minutes before the press conference started, he was going to have a *very* bad time of it. He managed just a single step before a hand caught the crook of his elbow, tight enough to stop blood circulating.

"I might need help on the stairs."

They crossed the lot and entered the building at an old man's crawl, Carl occasionally jerking his arm but unable to loosen those ancient fingers. He recalled the Kanoska scene, the impression he'd had that Kahleskawe hadn't needed the chief's help at all, and thought again that this was a put-on; Kahleskawe had wound him up intentionally and was now slowing him down the same way. He had no idea *why* the old man would do this, but it was, as his throbbing bladder could attest, effective.

It was standing room only when they finally got inside, and Carl recognized quite a few faces in the crowd: Barry the prick; Jennifer Pullet, from *The Herald*; Tonya Freysinger, who'd just started at *The Eagle-Tribune* when Carl had had his *troubles* and now had his old job. There were others, from TV and print across the country, all watching him stroll up the side-aisle almost late, an ancient whacko clamped to his arm like the world's ugliest prom date.

Terrific.

Barry spoke to the woman beside him and they laughed, she discreetly looking away, him staring at Carl.

I hope you die of something really embarrassing, Carl thought. Barry gave him a grinning thumbs-up. Carl gave him the finger, turned away—and nearly collied with Police Chief Tuckwa.

"What are you doing here?"

A group of suits stood behind the chief—the town council, perhaps?—plus two men lurking a little apart, matching dark suits, haircuts, sunglasses, and white skin all marking them as the feds in charge of the investigation. Tuckwa must have been on his way to the low stage at the front of the room, seen Carl, and detoured over just for him.

Well, well, he thought. *This'll give people something to talk about. Eat it, Barry.*

Carl cocked his head with a grin. "Now, Chief, this is a *press conference*, remember? You should. You called it. And I *am* the press." He hooked a thumb under the ID dangling from his breast pocket and gave it a little bounce. "Remember?"

"I'm not talking to you." Tuckwa shouldered past Carl so hard he might have staggered had Kahleskawe's iron grip not steadied him. The chief stood almost nose-to-nose with the old didanawisgi, and Carl saw the family resemblance, blurred in Kahleskawe through decades of life.

The chief's lips hardly moved, and Carl, not two feet away, barely heard him. "What are you doing here?"

"I know things you must know." Kahleskawe's rusty, old man's voice was strong, and the crowd—reporters all, after a fashion—quieted down to listen.

"I'll come to your trailer later," Tuckwa murmured. "Go watch your stories. I'll be there when I can."

"I know things you must know *now*." The old man's volume was rising, much to the joy of the listening crowd.

The louder Kahleskawe grew, the quieter Tuckwa became, speaking barely above a whisper. "If I wanted you here, I'd have picked you up." His head swiveled as if on gimbals, his gaze flowing down to the old man's hand, still gripping the reporter's elbow, then up until he was glaring at Carl. His voice rose a notch. "You brought him?"

Carl shrugged. "He was in my car when I woke up, asking for a ride. What was I supposed to do?"

"He just appeared in your car?"

"Actually . . ." Carl shrugged again. "Well, yeah."

"And where *was* your car?"

"What does it matter?" The line had worked for the old man, so why not? A smile finally touched Kahleskawe's lips, and that rough voice came again, its loudest yet.

"The press conference is about to start. Do you expect an old man to stand, or—"

A uniformed officer had already appeared behind Tuckwa bearing an extra chair. Carl recognized the cop who'd dropped off the Kanoska press briefing, and this time clocked the nameplate pinned to his pocket: *Ahoka*.

"Here you go, sir." Officer Ahoka planted the chair right behind Kahleskawe where he stood. "You can have a seat and we can get this—"

"May I not sit up front?" the old man bugled. "My eyes are old."

But they see, Carl finished silently. From the look on his face, Tuckwa wasn't buying the Methuselah act either, but short of tossing the old man out, there was little he could do. Ahoka looked at his boss. Tuckwa glanced at the seated crowd—the whole room taking in the press conference pre-show, waiting to see what he'd say—and gave a disgusted wave.

"Fine."

Moving with alacrity—Carl marked him down as a people pleaser—Ahoka carried the chair up and placed it at the end of the front row.

"Please," Kahleskawe said, tugging Carl's elbow and gesturing for his human cane to help him to the front of the room. A strangled cough drew Carl's gaze, and he saw the chief's cop face had finally cracked; the expression beneath said, quite clearly, *Are you fucking kidding me?*

"Hey." Carl shrugged, ancient prom date on his arm. "He's *your* great-grandfather."

Tuckwa's eyes narrowed before the cop face slid seamlessly back into place. Hand knotted tightly about his arm, Kahleskawe led Carl to the chair and sat as the chief and his suited retinue took the stage. Carl started to step away, praying to find a bathroom before searching out a spot where he could lean on a wall somewhere, but that damned claw jerked him back.

"May my driver have a chair as well?"

Up at the podium, the chief's expression didn't change, but Carl could see the effort it was taking. Ahoka was suddenly beside Carl with another chair, like some furniture-specialized genie. Carl glanced toward the back of the room where Barry the prick sat, gave him a little wave and a thumbs-up, and took a seat.

"You really are good at this," he murmured from the side of his mouth, and the old man gave a dry, self-satisfied "Ha!"

Chief Charlie's flat tones suddenly boomed from the speakers above the stage. "Ladies and gentlemen, let's get started. My name is Charles Tuckwa, and I'm chief of the Cherokee, North Carolina branch of the Qualla Boundary Tribal Police. Wednesday, at approximately four forty-five pm, a person or persons unknown attacked and killed George Robert Kanoska, age eight, while the boy played in the unpurposed land beside his home." He quickly recapped the crime, covering what Carl had already read in the press release. "We've canvassed the area, and no one recalls seeing anyone entering or leaving that unpurposed lot during the period of time we're interested in. Now, if we missed anyone"—*Fat chance of that*, Carl thought, *two thousand people and he knows every one*—"or someone we've already spoken to remembers something, even if it seems insignificant, we'd like them to call the station."

He paused, gazing out at the listening crowd, though he didn't bother looking Carl's way.

Or was he avoiding his great-grandfather?

"Then, on Thursday morning, sometime between four and six am, while Lillian Anne Ghigooie, age twelve, was fishing before school, a person or persons unknown attacked her as well. She was found by her father, William Ghigooie, who'd gone looking for her after receiving a call from the school letting him know she'd been absent that day.

"Similarities between the crimes suggest they may have been committed by the same person or persons, but we have nothing definitive. In both cases a knife was used, but forensic examination of the wounds has been inconclusive. There was no evidence of sexual molestation, and the killers left nothing behind: no fingerprints, blood, or any tissue. This might look like extreme caution, but the children were also simply alone and away from their homes, suggesting crimes of opportunity rather than any planned attack. There is nothing to indicate these children were stalked, or lured into a safety-compromised situation. We are asking that the people of Cherokee keep their kids close for a while, maybe a little closer than usual, while we do our jobs."

"Chief Tuckwa!" someone called out from the other side of the room. "Is this the first Native American serial killer?"

Chief Tuckwa pushed out his palms. "Hold on, there. We're not even sure these crimes are connected. This is—"

"But aren't those two men behind you," the woman beside Barry the prick called out, "agents from the Federal Behavioral Crimes Unit? Serial killer hunters, in other words?"

There was a rumble from the press pool and the chief actually looked startled. "What? No! No, these are—" He stepped away from the podium, speaking to the group behind him. The Caucasian bookends stood.

"Ladies and gentlemen," said the one who took the mic. "We're Special Agents Maurice Howard and Lawrence Fine with the Bureau of Indian Affairs. Since the Qualla Boundary is a federal reservation, the BIA is required to maintain a presence at any major crime investigation. It's purely protocol, and we're just here assisting Chief Tuckwa."

He started to step away from the mic, but Barry's friend piped up again. "So, this *isn't* a serial killer, despite such obvious similarities between the murders?"

Special Agent Howard wore a small, patient smile. "Even if we wanted to, we couldn't classify these crimes as *serial killings*. Title Eighteen, United States Code, Chapter Fifty-One, Section 1111 states that 'the term *serial killings* means a series of three or more killings,' so whether they're connected or not, the phrase simply doesn't apply here."

Panic flowed into Carl's chest like a cold wind through an open window. *What do you mean it doesn't apply? If there's no serial killer, I have no story!*

Just the phrase *serial killer* sold papers. Even if he broke a story about kids being murdered by the oldest man in the world, he'd just be the oldest *man*, not the oldest *serial killer*! Not the first verified Native American *serial killer*! If Kahleskawe was relegated to just another old man who'd snapped on a couple of kids, that was just a *decent* story, even for *The Weekly World Mirror*. Without the serial killer angle, it wasn't what Carl needed to catapult himself out of the tabloids and back where he belonged. At that thought, voices sounded in his head.

Barry the prick: *Not a real paper, you mean?*

The kid, Connor: *That comic book thing I see at the supermarket checkout?*

Chief Charlie Tuckwa: *You still have your scoop on all the real papers.*

Max, his smug boss with his smug chin: *As far as anybody out there in the real world is concerned, this is where you belong.*

Carl Spaberg: *Oh, fuck* that *noise!*

Special Agent Howard stepped back again, but Carl suddenly found himself on his feet. "What about the Soco Construction site, on Monday?"

The agents paused, shared a glance, then continued to their seats, Howard motioning Tuckwa toward the mic. Apparently, *this* question couldn't be answered with a glib, U.S. Code recitation: Police Chief Tuckwa had just been handed the bag, in case they needed to leave someone holding it.

"Monday's incident, though tragic, was a completely separate incident perpetrated by an extremist environmental group, with no children involved. We are looking into that in a separate—"

"Has any group," Carl called, "come forward to claim credit?"

"No."

Tuckwa was all cop face; there were bricks with more expression. Carl knew the chief was thinking about their phone conversation the previous evening. He'd been right about Carl looking out for his own best interests; his mistake had been thinking he understood where those interests lay.

"And you're discounting the similarities there?"

Everyone had gone quiet. Carl realized with a jolt he'd actually taken the lead in questioning the officials on the case. A whole room filled with journalists and reporters, all sitting back and listening to a writer from the God-damned *Weekly World Mirror*.

Because I'm Carl-fucking-Spaberg, and don't you forget it.

"According to the BIA investigation of the Soco Construction scene," said Tuckwa, causing the special agents to sit up straight behind him, "there *are* no similarities."

The agents had left Tuckwa holding the bag, but the police chief had deftly handed it back. Chief Charlie's flat, matter-of-fact manner would give that statement undeniable weight when the TV newsies threw it in front of millions of Americans as a ready-made soundbite.

Bravo, Chief. You may not be the local yokel I took you for. Carl paused, giving the moment the emphasis it deserved, half expecting someone else to jump in. A heartbeat passed. Carl still had the floor.

It was entirely possible he was getting an erection.

"Then maybe we should be talking to the special agents in residence. Agents Howard and Fine, wasn't a knife also used at the construction site Monday?"

Tuckwa stepped back as Special Agent Howard retook the mic and cleared his throat. "Knives are the most common weapon used in assaults in this area, rather than the gunshot wounds you may be used to hearing about in the big city. It's a useful tool for many of the more rural jobs, and just about everyone here carries one. Merely the fact that a blade or blades were used on Monday is not significant."

His voice had more bounce now, was a little more *car-salesman-y*, trying to sound more friendly for the cameras. A mistake, Carl thought: after Tuckwa's phlegmatic delivery, the fed sounded like a huckster.

"There were no children involved, and as Chief Tuckwa stated, we believe it was an ecologically-purposed group aiming to—"

"What about the harvesting, Agent Howard?"

The agent blinked. "Beg your pardon?"

A quiet rumble went through the press pool, half questioning, the other half shushing.

"The harvesting? Of their livers?"

Howard went as stone-faced as the chief, but it was too much, too late: such a departure from his assumed joviality merely underlined the agent's discomfort.

"There were some, ah, *excisions*, at the construction site, but we're still waiting on the full forensics report on that."

"You're referring to the removal of the victims' livers on Monday. What about the Kanoska and Ghigooie children, on Wednesday and Thursday? Their livers had been excised as well." Carl spread his hands. "*Connection?*"

The rumble returned. Special Agent Howard wheeled to glare at Chief Tuckwa. Tuckwa met his gaze calmly, though Carl thought a slight smile touched the edges of that hard slash the man called a mouth. There was an instant of silent communication—Carl imagined Howard saying *I thought you said he was under control?* while the chief replied *I told you he was a dick*—and then Howard snapped back to the mic, his face the expressionless mask they'd probably issued him with his federal ID and sidearm.

"There is, as yet, no official connection between the Soco Construction case and the attacks on these children. We will keep you apprised of any—"

"So, what, you're just going to wait for him to strike again"—so wrapped up was he in getting this thing blown up into the career-saving fuckarow he needed, for a horrified instant Carl had *almost* pointed at Kahleskawe, but caught himself—"before you call this what it is and give the situation the attention and resources it deserves?"

"She has already struck again!"

This shout nearly sent Carl staggering in surprise. Beside him, Thomas Kahleskawe had shot to his feet, apparently forgetting, in his agitation, to even pretend to need Carl's arm. Up on the podium, Carl saw both Howard and Tuckwa mouth two words precisely in unison: *Oh, shit.*

Kahleskawe stepped forward. "She has struck again, somewhere on the mountain! This is what I came to tell you. Last night, under the cover of dark, she struck. She fed. I heard! I heard the thunder!"

The audience erupted in a tumult, fifty reporters all asking their questions at once.

"Who's the old guy?"

"Where are these new victims?"

"What else haven't you told us? What are you hiding?"

Amidst the sudden row, Carl found himself trying to grasp what *might* have been a memory prodded by Kahleskawe's words. *Didn't I hear thunder last night? Right while I was looking up at the clear sky? I can almost . . .*

Officer Ahoka appeared, looking like he wanted to do something but wasn't sure what. He glanced to the podium, seeking guidance from above—a higher police official, if not a higher power—but Chief Tuckwa was already on his way down the three stairs to the floor, coming to take charge of his great-grandfather and further cementing the bag firmly in the grip of the BIA man still at the mic. Agent Howard's voice boomed out across the room.

"Ladies and gentlemen, *please*! I don't know where this, uh, *gentleman* is getting his information, but I assure you, there have been no new casualties. We're not *hiding* anything, and I resent that implication."

"Just the liver harvesting," someone shouted, close enough to the stage that the mic picked it up. Howard looked to the chief, desperate to hand off the situation.

"Chief Tuckwa? Would you come up here, please?"

But the chief was face-to-face with his great-grandfather again. He was making a shooing gesture with both hands, urging the ancient didanawisgi toward the exit, but the old man stood firm, yammering at his great-grandson in nonstop Cherokee.

Special Agent Howard dialed up his command tone, almost shouting into the mic to be heard over the crowd, despite the amplification. "Chief Tuckwa! Would you please come up here and control your people!"

Oh, Carl thought. *'Your people.' That's gonna play* great *on the news, paleface.*

The chief offered Agent Howard an over-the-shoulder *wait a minute*, at which the fed actually sputtered. Carl kind of hoped Howard would keep nagging; he had no idea what Kahleskawe was saying, but Charlie Tuckwa's face had darkened from his usual healthy bronze to a dangerous-looking brick, and Carl didn't think it would take much more to get the chief to blow. People said all *kinds* of interesting things when tempers flared, and more and more scarlet flowed into Tuckwa's cheeks as the ancient Cherokee shouted.

Jesus Christ, he's an actual redskin!

From the outer edges of the seating area, Carl had the angle to see two new uniforms enter the back of the auditorium, a man and a woman. Both looked young, and resembled spooked horses around the eyes. The two started toward the chief, *excuse me*-ing their way past folks crowding in the aisle. When they saw he was standing nose-to-nose with Kahleskawe, the man wisely held back while the young lady pressed forward, obviously in dire need of the chief of police.

This might be the stick of dynamite that makes the volcano blow.

Most people, seeing the imminent explosion of another human being, might have backed away so as not to be caught up in the emotional blast radius. But Carl was, first and foremost, a newsman: he stayed put and raised his phone, hoping to get a picture.

"Chief Tuckwa?"

Tuckwa made the over-the-shoulder gesture again, this time aimed at his fellow officer, but the young woman, possibly unable to see the frightening shade of the chief's face, was not deterred. "Chief!"

Tuckwa wheeled. "*What*?" It was the first time Carl had heard the chief raise his voice, and it was a good one. The bellow rang out, and every reporter in the room realized something juicy was happening, and shut up to hear. It was into this sudden quiet that the round-eyed officer shouted "We got another one!"

Forget hearing a pin drop: you could have heard a needle feeling tired. Chief Tuckwa took a breath, then another, getting control of himself with a rapidity Carl found both impressive and disappointing, though he took advantage of the moment to stare at Kahleskawe in wonder.

Holy shit, he knew! *Before anyone else, when only the killer could have known, he* knew! Carl had been convincing himself before, talking himself into his own story, but now?

I can't believe I picked the real serial killer out of the crowd! Christ, I might actually be as good as I think I am!

The officer, feeling the scrutiny of every eye in the place, suddenly looked self-conscious. "Sorry, Chief, but you turned off your cell and you're not near a radio. You said you wanted to know if—"

A raised finger halted her words, and though Tuckwa—fully under control again—tried to be quiet, he'd lost any vocal camouflage he'd once had from the crowd. "There's another child?"

"Two." It was almost a whisper, but her raised finger V left no doubt. "And their father."

Tuckwa thrust a palm toward her in a *halt right there.* "Hang on, Officer Catawnee. This isn't the place for—"

But Catawnee was bursting with news, and not to be denied. "But Chief! There's a survivor! The mom! *We've got a witness!*"

There was a two-second count of absolute silence as the chief—and the rest of the room—digested this. Then the noise came back like a cymbal crash. Questions flew. Special Agent Howard tapped the mic, calling, "Attention, please!"

Without looking away from Officer Catawnee, Tuckwa snapped out a hand and caught Kahleskawe's shoulder. Though it had been happening right in front of him, Carl had missed the old man taking an unobtrusive step away, sliding quietly toward the nearest exit. But Tuckwa had seen, and if that grip Kahleskawe had used on Carl earlier was hereditary, the old man was caught tighter than if he'd been handcuffed. Tuckwa leaned close to his great-grandfather's ear, and his lips formed the words *You're with me*. He looked up, saw Carl standing close and watching, and raised his voice to be heard.

"And you're not."

He waved for Officer Catawnee and her partner to follow, then turned and began marching Kahleskawe toward the front of the room, lifting his waving hand to gesture toward Howard, still tapping the mic and calling for order. He flicked a finger in a circle, then pointed toward the exit behind the small stage: *Wrap this fiasco up and meet me out back.*

"Ladies and gentlemen," Howard said to the unlistening room. "Thank you for giving us your time here today. We'll keep you apprised as the situation develops. Thank you."

With a squeal and click, the BIA man turned off the microphone, collected his partner from the gaggle of suits at the back of the stage, and headed off to meet the chief and his charge. Carl watched them go, the crowd milling about as reporters and townspeople alike swirled for the doors.

Son of a bitch, I actually did it! I don't even have to make anything up this time. I actually got the guy! And he wants to talk to me!

He desperately looked around.

Now where's the fucking bathroom?

Crime Might Pay

Fssst. Clink.

"What a prick."

After the press conference, Carl had followed along to the new crime scene: Mile-High Camp Ground, up in the mountains. There, he'd run into a little difficulty. *Mirror* stories didn't tend to track along with more mainstream news outlets, so over the past year, Carl had gotten rather used to being the only press at whatever dance he was attending. He'd been the only out-of-towner, the only *reporter*, in Cherokee for most of the week. Alone, he'd snuck into (*infiltrated*, he mentally amended) the Kanoska scene. Working solo, he'd managed to get around the uniforms guarding the Ghigooie scene as well.

Here, though, there was a lot more clear space than there had been at the Ghigooie scene, making sneaking inherently more difficult. Couple that with the fact that, unlike then, today he was part of a group, and he'd found it impossible to do a slow fade. Alone, he might have wandered about and eventually slipped from police awareness as they became involved with the scene; in a group, however, he was always noticed as *leaving the group*, drawing eyes to him exactly when he least wanted them.

And then there had been Barry.

Carl tipped the bottle. Swallowed. Belched. "The prick."

Standing there looking at an oiled dirt intersection with its worn bathhouse, piled up outside the yellow tape with the rest of them, Barry had entertained himself by needling

117

Carl—which had, again, called attention to Carl right when he'd least wanted it.

"Hey, tabloid, what was all that stuff you were spouting back there about livers?"

"Can't remember my name, Barry? No wonder your stories are so factually inconsistent."

The prick's lips had shaped a sarcastic O of surprise. "Ooooh! The tabloid guy's talking about 'factual inconsistencies!' How many *facts*"—he dropped finger quotes around the word—"did you guys have for that 'Bigfoot in suburbia' story? Or that whole 'rat girl' series?" He grinned. "Or your 'Monsters in Main' p—"

"You know all those? You must be a fan! Did you bring a copy? I could sign it for you."

Some of the crowd had raised their eyebrows at that, and the jerk actually got flustered.

"Hey! I don't *read* those things! I see the headlines at the checkout counter, just like everybody el—"

"He has a point." It was the woman who'd been sitting beside Barry, who'd jumped in with questions of her own before Carl had grabbed center stage. "*Somewhere* in there. What *were* you saying about the kids' livers?"

The crowd had quieted again—all except Barry, still sputtering about people thinking he'd stoop to reading *trash*—but Carl didn't get that same heady surge he'd felt spearheading the questions at the press conference. He'd gotten past the rush of having a roomful of mainstream reporters—all of whom, he knew, thought they were better than him—*listening* to him, treating him as at *least* a colleague.

During his drive into the mountains, he'd recalled Tuckwa's words: *They break that story and you lose your edge, right?*

Dammit, the chief *was* right. Carl *had* to stop underestimating the man. This wasn't holding the cops in the hotseat to get the story anymore. Answering questions *now* would simply be handing his story off to the competition—which was, technically, what he'd been doing during the press conference anyway: an idiot, swept up in the moment, impressed with his own cleverness.

But I had *to do that*, he thought, meeting the woman's expectant gaze. *If they hadn't started calling it a serial killing, I'd have lost the story.*

Of course, right after he'd shared this tidbit with all the other reporters in town and soured his already shaky relationship with the local cops, the report had come in about *this* killing, cementing the serial killer angle anyway.

The idea that he might not be *quite* as smart as he thought he was danced around the outskirts of Carl's consciousness, but his subconscious grabbed it before it could cross into the forefront of his mind and shoved it into a cell in the deepest, darkest portion of his brain. He didn't have time for thoughts like that now. He'd just lock it away and pull it out for inspection later, when he had less pressure. Like after he retired. Or maybe when he was dead.

Right now, though, he needed damage control. His questioner still waited; his thought-gathering pause had gone on long enough that even Barry was paying attention again. He raised an eyebrow and tried for haughty.

"And you are . . . ?"

"Lindsey Thomas, *New York Post*."

No wonder Barry'd been sucking up to her; the *Post* had twice the circulation of the *Boston Globe*. Carl noticed she didn't ask his name. She and Barry had been talking as he'd entered the press conference, the prick quite likely telling her of Carl's downfall, the story Barry simply never tired of.

Terrific.

"Well, Lindsey, I'm not going to do your job for you."

"A little late for that, if what you said earlier pans out. You sure you don't want to confirm it for me? You know"–she smiled, a slick combination of mockery and flirtation—"sort of *go all the way*?"

"Nope."

"He can't confirm shit," Barry piped up, trying to recover lost ground. "When you just make stuff up for a living, you don't *need* confirmation."

"*Christ*, Barry. If you can't confirm this on your own, you don't *deserve—*"

"It's been confirmed." One of the officers assigned to keep them out had been listening. "The local BIA office released a statement. They weren't happy about it getting out. They're probably trying to get ahead of it."

Barry went red in the face (*An aneurysm*, Carl prayed, *please, God, make it an aneurysm*) while Lindsey simply arched an eyebrow.

Carl shrugged. "I'm the best."

He'd spent a couple of hours standing the line, hoping the cops would let something slip, waiting for a statement from the chief, Barry yakking at him the whole time. Responding to the prattling dickhead wouldn't have gotten him anywhere, but the constant references to Carl as *tabloid* were getting under his skin, and the second time Barry had started the tale of Carl's fateful "Monsters in Maine" story, he'd had enough.

Anything Tuckwa says will be on the record, he'd rationalized, driving out of the campground. *I'll hear it later. Besides, Tuckwa's so pissed at me right now, he probably won't say anything if I'm there.*

So here he was, sitting in his room at the Super 8, with a six pack of trash can Heinekens to help him think. *I'm much better off avoiding the pack. Got a lot done before they even started showing up. I'll do a shit-ton more if I can just stay solo, like before.*

"Lone Wolf Spaberg." He chucked the empty bottle in the waste can beside his chair—he'd scored a spare from the front desk—and pulled a freshie from the ice.

Okay, that has absolutely no ring to it, but the plan's still good.

And whatever he was going to do, he'd have to move on it. At one point, the prick had asked, "Hey, tabloid, who was that old man you walked in with? The one who started spouting off about thunder?"

Carl had turned on the bullshit machine. "Streetcorner doomsayer. He was in the parking lot shouting 'The end is nigh!' and latched onto my arm like a leech, so I had to bring him in with me. Got me a seat up front, though, didn't it?"

"You two looked awfully chummy. Yes, sir, *awfully* chummy."

Carl had rolled his eyes. "Okay, Barry, you got me. That was the Cherokee Slasher trying to turn himself in to the police." He'd fluttered his fingers in a scooting gesture. "Why don't you run along and try to verify *that* while we grownups wait to hear from the cops."

A few people had chuckled, and Barry had gone sputtery again, but not *everyone* had laughed it off. He wouldn't put it past anyone in that crowd—not even Barry—to get around to looking into Thomas Kahleskawe. Maybe sooner than later. He was going to have to push, to make something happen.

"But *what*?" A second empty joined the first, and *fssst-clink*, he slouched back in his chair and kept thinking.

They've got a witness, but who knows what she saw. The best thing . . . Hell, I might as well reach for the stars if I'm making a wish list. The best thing for me—a real TV and movie gotcha *moment—would be for this witness to pick Kahleskawe out of a lineup. But with the chief protecting him, Kahleskawe won't ever stand in a lineup—and even if I could, somehow, manage to get Chief Tuckwa to put ole great-grampy and the witness together, there's no way he'd ever let me be there with my camera . . .*

The thought trailed off, the bottle touching his lips though not tilted enough to drink. A thought churned around and through the cogs and wheels inside his skull, an idea going through once then turning about to come through again so he could see it from both sides.

"Wait a minute . . ."

He poked at the idea for holes, any indication it was merely beer-induced brilliance, the kind of thing he'd look back on while hung over and wonder just what the hell he'd been thinking. But—

"It just might work!" He grabbed his phone, scrolled to a number, and punched SEND.

"Officer Nelawe! So good to hear your voice. I wanted to ask . . . Well, yes, the chief *did* ask me not to . . . Technically, I *didn't* blab about it. I asked Special Agent Howard, and *he* . . . Look, I'm sorry you feel that way, but that's no reason to—Hello? Shit."

The press conference was already biting him in the ass. *Well, it wasn't like they were being all that helpful before, was it? There's got to be some way to—Wait!* He scrolled through his phone to another number. *I need to call them anyway, and they probably know where—*

"Hello, Ben? Carl Spaberg here. I understand you and Sam rolled out to the Mile High Campground this morning? Great! Listen, it turns out I do have more questions for you two. If we could meet somewhere, we could . . . Really? Oh, that's a shame. I was going to make it worth your while, but if you can't . . . Well, the *Weekly World Mirror* is definitely not above *paying* for your assistance, *especially* since you'd be taking time away from your regular work. But I understand if you . . . Oh, you can? Wonderful! Think you can take a break in about a half hour? Okay, where? Perfect! I'll talk to you then."

He disconnected the call, made sure to grab his wallet, then stood and ran the idea through his head again. It looked solid. Risky—and wasn't risk an element in all the best plans?—but with a solid outcome for him if he played it right.

"This is going to *work*!"

SUNDAY

Your Ride, Sir

"It's open!"

Carl opened the door and stood in the doorway, hoping some fresh air would come in with him, maybe mitigate the smell a little.

"Mr. Kahleskawe?" he belted out in a voice far too cheerful to be his own. "Are you ready?"

The old man, already sunk deep into that shapeless couch in front of that huge TV, turned, squinting, blinded by the morning brightness streaming in around his visitor. "Ready? Ready for what?"

"Your appointment."

"What appointment?"

Carl had heard of people *burbling*, so he gave it a shot. What came out sounded more maniacal than reassuring, but Kahleskawe didn't quite struggle when Carl stepped forward and *helped* him off the couch. "Oh, *you* re*mem*ber! Your appointment with Doctor Rmble-*cough*!"

Carl was a few inches taller than Kahleskawe, and used his height to advantage, crowding close once he had the old man standing, giving him a terrific view of a blue shirt with its badge and nametag, hoping the stethoscope draping his neck would capture and hold those old but seeing eyes for just a few seconds. He turned Kahleskawe toward the door, scooting in behind him, ostensibly balancing and bracing the old man while speedily patting him down. He'd come in unannounced and moving fast, so unless the ancient psychopath sat around packing blades all the time, Carl thought he should have caught him unarmed. He didn't find anything, but he *was* moving fast, and trying to be surreptitious, *and* not exactly trained in patting people down. He was going to have to chance it.

"Come along, sir!" he chirped—actually *chirped*—hustling the old man toward the door.

"I have no shoes!"

"Don't need 'em."

"But I don't recall any appointment!"

"You don't have to! That's why we're here."

They exited to the tiny porch, Kahleskawe throwing up an arm to protect his eyes from the sudden sun. Carl half-carried him down the three steps, aware once more the man's spindly frame was heavier than it looked. His rental was parked right at the foot of the stairs, engine running, passenger's door open, and he had Kahleskawe inside the car before those squinting, watering eyes could register what it was. In a flash, the old man was belted in, the car door slammed, and Carl was flinging himself behind the wheel. The tires spat gravel as he pulled a quick U-turn and headed up the drive to the road.

"This is not an ambulance." Kahleskawe's eyes had adjusted, and he was looking about in a kind of wonder. "And you are not an ambulance man."

Carl glanced down at his *uniform*: light blue work shirt and navy slacks, just like Sam and Ben wore, along with the costume badge and borrowed stethoscope.

"Well spotted."

"And there is no appointment I've forgotten. You have kidnapped me." Kahleskawe leaned a little closer. "You really are good at this."

Carl had expected yelling and fighting, and had planned accordingly; this calm acceptance of the situation was a little unnerving.

Did I miss a blade on his belt or something?

The thought that he might have kidnapped an *armed* serial killer who was just waiting for the car to stop so he could go all Jack the Ripper felt a little like a gut punch. Unable to get *close* to burbling with that thought in mind, he offered up a tight smile. "Well, you *do* have a meeting, and it *is* at the hospital. Don't worry, though. I need you to remain calm, okay?"

Before Kahleskawe could respond, Carl jabbed a syringe into the old man's thigh and depressed the plunger.

"Aaiee! What did you doooaalumph—"

Kahleskawe's sharp eyes rolled and closed, and he collapsed forward to hang loosely in the shoulder harness, the ketamine shoving him off to dreamland before he could even finish his question.

Carl said, "Thanks, Ben," though Ben had no idea he'd supplied Carl with any drugs. At their meeting the previous afternoon, Carl had asked for a tour of the ambulance transporting so many news-breaking bodies, "Just to get a feel for it, for when I write you two up." He'd moved fast and rummaged quickly, using his body to block any view of his hands, and found the K just before they asked him to get off the bus. He'd turned to them with a stethoscope in one hand, asking if he could borrow it to complete his disguise and

127

distracting them from noticing his other hand pocketing the ampule.

The meeting had gone well, resulting in a detailed description of the ambulance entrance of the Cherokee Indian Hospital, where yesterday's survivor—one Margaret Messing—was currently under observation. It had been easy enough to convince the boys of the veracity of his plan to sneak into the hospital to get an exclusive interview with the survivor. He *did* mean to sneak in to see the Messing woman; he'd just failed to mention he wouldn't be making the trip alone.

It had cost Carl a hundred bucks—*each*—but Sam and Ben had promised to do a little snooping. This morning, the investment had borne fruit: Ben had called to say Margaret Messing was in room 217, and there was no guard in the hallway that they could see.

So, all I have to do is get to the hospital, slap this guy on a gurney, go in through the ambulance entrance, and head up to room 217. Introduce myself to Messing, get my camera ready, and whip off the sheet covering the patient *I'm transporting. The reaction when she sees the face of the man who just murdered her family will beat the pants off any old lineup identification. And the picture!*

He glanced at the wrinkled old face beside him; the unconscious Kahleskawe drooled copiously into his own lap.

Let's see the chief get him out of this one. Let's see him get himself *out of this one!*

"There will be questions, Chief. Oh, yes, there will. And Carl-fucking-Spaberg will be right there asking the tough ones!"

He passed a sign reading *Hospital 1-mi*, and grinned.

Visiting Hours, Schmisiting Hours

The gurney squealed along the door-lined hall, one wibble-wobbling wheel setting up a racket like it was *trying* to call attention to them.

Jesus Christ. Carl grit his teeth, keeping his head down. *Isn't it always the way?*

Though Sam had mentioned cast-aside and left-behind gurneys like the ambulance entrance would be choked with them, Carl had found only one. He'd had to move quickly, before someone came along and saw he was loading in a patient from his personal car, but now regretted his haste as they screeched along the otherwise silent corridor. He was scanning ahead, looking for another gurney to transfer the old man to, when a door opened and someone stepped into the hall. Carl looked down at Kahleskawe's sleeping face, avoiding eye contact so aggressively he didn't even see whether it was a man or woman.

Come on, come on! he thought. *How far is it to the damned elevator?*

"Hey! Hold up!"

It had been a man, and he did *not* sound happy. For an instant, Carl considered plunging ahead, running deeper into the hospital, wielding the old man like a squealing, wibble-wobbling battering ram, but he wasn't even sure where he was going. He stopped and lifted his head. *It was a good plan. It should have worked.*

The man loomed beside him. "Where do you think you're going with *that*?"

Carl decided to follow his strengths and try browbeating. "Okay, look! I—"

But the guy dropped to one knee. He pulled a can of WD-40 from somewhere and, guarding the floor from overspray with a rag, expertly applied the lubricant to the complaining wheel. He stood.

"Try it now."

Carl shoved the gurney. It rolled smooth and soundless, like pushing a cloud.

"There you go," said the man in the custodial coverall. "What would you guys do without us guys around to take care of your shit?"

"Uh, thanks?"

"No problem, buddy." But the custodian was talking to Carl's back, the reporter throwing a wave over one shoulder as he kept the suddenly silent stretcher in motion; he'd spotted the elevator at the end of the corridor. He hit the call button and the doors slid open with a sharp *ding*, the lift empty and inviting. Carl wheeled the recumbent Kahleskawe in like he'd been doing it for years and punched the two.

This is so going to work!

The elevator rose, and the doors opened on a slightly different corridor. Still white and empty, still a line of rooms to either side, but these were patient rooms; the doorframes had been painted a cheerful blue, and each sported a small plaque jutting from the top showing a room number to help visiting friends and family find where they were going.

Helpful to investigative reporters, too.

The rooms to either side nearest the elevator were marked *229* and *230*, the numbers diminishing ahead. Halfway down to the other end of the hall, where Carl could see what looked like a nurses' station, was the little plaque he was looking for: *217*. He activated his recorder app, dropped the phone onto the pillow beside Kahleskawe's head, and started the gurney rolling again, quietly narrating the scene for future write-up.

"The intrepid reporter makes his way down the final corridor. Only a single door stands between himself and salvation. In mere moments, he'll instigate the confrontation that will clear his name! Oh, the ignorant have ignored his talent, have mocked him, but this . . . this'll show all those sons of bitches that I'm Carl-fucking-Sp—*oh, shit*."

Coming around the corner from the nurses' station, a man had appeared, walking with a serious *I've-got-shit-to-do* stride, speaking into his cell phone in hard, flat tones.

"I don't care what newspaper or channel they say they're from. Nobody gets in here to bother the Messing woman, Ahoka, *especially* before we get some kind of coherent statement. Do you understand? I . . ."

Carl lowered his head again, letting the gurney float to a silent stop, and as the words trailed off and the footsteps slowed, he squeezed his eyes shut in a childish reflex: *If I can't see him, maybe he can't see me.*

"I'll call you back."

Carl held his breath.

"What the fuck are you doing here?"

Carl let his breath out and opened his eyes. *Two thousand residents and he knows them all—of course he recognizes me.*

"Good morning, Chief Tuckwa."

So Busted

"I asked you a question."

The chief moved to meet him, steps considered and slow. *Jesus Christ, he's stalking me*, Carl thought, more aware than ever that the police chief wore a gun.

"What the fuck are you doing here?" Tuckwa placed a hand on the foot of the gurney, staring down at its occupant. "No, let me rephrase that: What the fuck are you doing here *with my great-grandfather?*" His eyes came up, met Carl's own, and he touched his gun butt. "If you've hurt him—"

"Don't be an idiot." Carl raised his hands, showing they were empty—but also pulling Tuckwa's attention up, away from the uncovered phone still catching every word. "I was just bringing Mr. Kahleskawe in for a quick meeting, and—"

"Meeting? With who? What the hell are you talking about?"

The phone *was* capturing every word, and he hadn't been shot—yet—and if he was, well, they were already in the hospital, weren't they?

Time to make the story, and make it good—this might be for posterity.

Ignoring his frightened urge to crouch and offer a smaller target, Carl stood tall. His voice warbled only slightly.

"I'm bringing the Cherokee Butcher to face his victim."

"What the hell are . . . ? *The Cherokee Butcher?*"

Carl sketched an airy wave. "I'm trying it out. I haven't really decided *what* I'm going to call him. Now, stand aside—unless you're going to *protect* him again?"

Tuckwa's face was reddening. "Protect him? And you think he's . . . ? Do you know how *old* . . . ? *Have you lost your mind*?"

"*Someone* around here certainly has! Maybe a *couple* of someones! You're done, Chief. There are bodies on the ground, and I'm blowing this thing wide open. The people have a right to know."

Tuckwa's eyes bulged. "'The people have a right to know'? *That's* your excuse for . . . doing *whatever* you're doing with an old man?" His hand dipped out of sight. Carl tensed, but instead of his gun, the chief brought up handcuffs. "You're coming with me."

Tuckwa started around the gurney, but Carl darted the other way, keeping the old man between them. "Take it easy there, Chief."

"You stop resisting arrest and I'll *think* about taking it easy. But if you've hurt my great-grandfather—"

"I am fine."

Carl and Tuckwa looked down at the man lying between them with matching expressions of surprise. Thomas Kahleskawe gazed up at them, eyes open and clear.

"*Agiduda*?" said Tuckwa. "Are you all right? Did he—"

"I am fine," the old man repeated. His eyes shifted to Carl. "He seems to have a talent for kidnapping."

"I'll make sure to mention it to the prosecutor." Tuckwa lurched into motion, but Carl danced around to Kahleskawe's feet. Jostled, the gurney rolled sideways a few inches. The old man barked something in Cherokee and Tuckwa stopped, looking down at his great-grandfather's upside-down visage.

"I am fine *now*, but I am one hundred and twenty-six years old. Falling to this floor would shatter my bones like glass. Stop and listen to this man, *vgilisi*. I, for one, would like to hear why I was so neatly taken from my home."

Tuckwa's gaze snapped up. "You broke into his *house*?"

"No! I knocked. He pretty much came with me on his own."

"On my own," Kahleskawe grumbled, "I would have worn shoes."

"Fine." The chief tucked his cuffs away and straightened, but there was no forgiveness in his eyes; those dark orbs promised consequences. "Tell us. You apparently think a one-hundred-twenty-six-year-old man is the . . . What did you call him? *The Cherokee Butcher*? Please"—he nodded his head, not in agreement, but with nervous, furious energy—"explain. I'm sure we'd *love* to hear it."

This wasn't the plan. Carl was *supposed* to get his gotcha moment on film, undeniable proof the old man was indeed a maniac of the first water, and *then* lay out his thought process: Hercule Poirot expounding on the workings of his *little gray cells*. He hadn't planned on doing it this way, but the chief was angry and packing.

Besides, he thought. *The phone's locked, but catching every word. He gets pissed, slips up, makes* any *kind of admission, and it's winging its way up to the cloud and there'll be nothing he can do about it.*

"Like I said the day we met, Chief, I was sent here to cover the Soco Construction killings. But the day I arrived, there was another slaying: George Kanoska, age eight. Same MO as the Soco site. Your great-grandfather was there, spouting weird talk about thunder as you hustled him from the scene. A lot of people working the case that day were affected by the scene, but not Mr. Kahleskawe, here."

"He's a hundred and twenty-six years old," said Tuckwa. "He fought in both world wars. He has seen some shit. And he wasn't on the inside dealing with the boy or his mother, was he?"

"Well . . . no. But it was obvious you didn't want him talking to me. So, of course, I went to talk to him. He gave me the whole *Spearfinger* rundown, that creepy fairy tale about serial killing and cannibalism which just *happens* to match *exactly* with what's going on here. And here's the really creepy thing, Chuck-Tuck: he honestly seems to believe this shit, has a whole theory about a thousand-year-old ogre coming back from the dead to eat children. That sound like he's entirely hooked up to you?"

"He should believe instead in an invisible sky-daddy looking down on his every move, ready to send him off to an eternal fire for having sexy thoughts about his neighbor's wife? Or maybe in the sky-daddy's son, sent down to live among us until we kill him, and then he rises from the grave? What, that story makes more sense because Jesus was only dead three days before coming back?"

"There's talk around town of your great-grandfather's deteriorating mental faculties," Carl said. "He's forgetting things, talking crazy. Sounds like Alzheimer's and the onset of dementia to me, and—"

"'Talk around town'? You mean back-fence gossip?"

"I talked to a few people." Okay, Ms. Oolootsa had talked to people, and Carl had merely spoken with the librarian, but Tuckwa didn't need his source.

"Were any of them his doctor? I doubt it. Dr. Cort wouldn't have told you a thing, but he *would* have told me you were asking. So, you took small town gossip instead of looking for any actual medical opinions." Tuckwa shook his head. "And you think *I'm* a hick. So, you think this feeble old man you're describing is also running around overpowering all these people? How?"

"There's nothing feeble about his hands," Carl said, recalling Kahleskawe's iron grip. "And these kids aren't being beaten to death, or strangled: they're being butchered with a blade. A *baby* with a straight razor can kill a person if they swing it right, and you said yourself he's had military training. He *was* at the Kanoska site, and he doesn't drive. What, he just happened to be strolling by, and—"

"I heard on my police scanner that something had happened, so I walked over to see." Thomas Kahleskawe's voice was calm, despite what Carl was saying about him. "The way is long, by the roads, but I have been walking these mountains since before there were cars, and do not need roads. The Kanoska home is only a mile from my own, as the crow flies."

Carl looked from great-grandfather to great-grandson. "He has ways of getting into places he shouldn't. He managed to appear inside my locked car while I was sleeping, and—"

"When I was a rookie right out of the academy, my great-grandfather asked me all kinds of questions. One was how a slim jim worked—you know, those things crooks and tow truck drivers use to get into locked cars? I made the mistake of telling him, and he went and made a hobby of it." Chief Tuckwa's voice took on an odd mix of embarrassment and pride. "You're not the only one who's found him in their locked vehicle waiting for a ride. That guy you have figured for an Alzheimer's patient is probably the most skilled car thief in the state who's never actually stolen a car. I keep confiscating his slim jims, but he always has another when he needs one."

The old man shrugged. "Amazon."

You've got to be kidding me. Giving up on all the little things—the stuff that would all seem so obvious once Kahleskawe's guilt had been established—Carl skipped to the end, to the point where he'd actually believed.

"You heard him yesterday. We *all* heard him yesterday. He knew the killer had struck again before your officers came in with the news. He knew before *anyone* knew—anyone but the killer, that is. That's the *only* way he could have known, and—"

"He was talking about *thunder*, you idiot! Signs and portents, not evidence or fact! You were right, we have a serial killer working here, one who seems to have the shortest cool-down period the feds have ever heard of. Saying 'I think he may have killed again' is *not* the same as saying 'Last night he sliced up three quarters of a nice tourist family in a campground bathroom'!"

Tuckwa turned away, running his hands through his hair. For a moment, Carl thought he might say something constructive. When he spun back, however, while not quite in the gunfighter's crouch Carl had seen in countless movies, Tuckwa suddenly looked aggressive again, and his hand *was* near his gun.

"That's it? That's all? And with just this, you broke into my great-grandfather's house—"

"I knocked!"

"—and dragged him all the way down here—"

"We drove!"

"—and *you* think I'm just gonna—"

"Excuse me." Between them, Thomas Kahleskawe's hand rose into the air like a school child in need of the bathroom.

"*What*?" Tuckwa snapped, then realized just who he was snapping *at*, and softened his tone. "What is it, *Agiduda*?"

The old man, who'd been lying flat, now lifted his head to look at Carl. "Why am I here?"

Carl felt his own face reddening. "Oh, for the love of— Weren't you listening? I *know* it's you, and I think the chief here knows it too, and has been—"

"Here. In this hospital. What did you want to do with me *here*? *Now*?"

"Oh! Uh—" Carl pointed to room 217, so close and yet so far away. "I was bringing you to that room right there. The survivor is in there, the woman who lost her family the other night. They said she's a witness. I want her to see you." His gaze shifted up to meet Tuckwa's. "I want her to look at his face, point her finger, and say it was him. No identification pack, no police lineup, no warning, no nothing. Just put him in front of her and see what she does."

And capture her response to share with my readers, he finished silently.

"Absolutely not," said Tuckwa.

"All right," said Kahleskawe.

They both looked at him in surprise again. Carl recovered first.

"Okay, let's go!"

He started pushing the gurney, but Tuckwa caught the other end and stopped it cold.

"No. No way."

Carl pushed harder. "Hiding something, Chief?"

"Excuse me?" A small woman in a nurse's uniform marched up the corridor with tiny, neat strides, emanating an authority that more than made up for her lack of physical stature; this lady wore the title *head nurse* like a suit of armor. Faces peered at them from the far end of the hall, nurses and orderlies curious about what was happening but unwilling to come down and possibly get caught in the middle of it.

"What the hell is going on here?"

"Just handling a situation," said Tuckwa. "I'm sorry for the commotion. I—"

"This is a *hospital*." Her quiet voice cut through Tuckwa's like a surgical scalpel. "Not your station house, Chief Tuckwa. You will keep your *situation* under control and quiet, or you will leave. Is that understood?" There was iron in her hair, eyes, and tone. She'd come up the hallway without any orderlies or physical backup, and Carl was certain it had never occurred to her that she might need any—no more than it had crossed her mind that the chief of police wouldn't leave the building if she wanted him to.

To be fair, it never crossed Carl's either.

"I'm sorry for the commotion," Tuckwa repeated. "It won't happen again."

"See that it doesn't." She raised a hand and pointed past the chief, pinning Thomas Kahleskawe with a stiffened finger. "And *you*. Behave yourself." She turned and started back toward the nurses' station, where the watching faces had already disappeared.

"Good to see you too, Bethany," Kahleskawe called, but the head nurse gave no indication she heard. The old man looked at his great-grandson, then the reporter. "Help me down from here, and let us get the visit started."

Carl moved to help the old man, but Tuckwa waved him off with an energy bordering on violence. "Fine! We'll do this, and you'll look like an idiot—even more than you do already—but you stay away from my great-grandfather."

Then keep your great-grandfather out of my car, Carl tactfully did not say.

The police chief helped Kahleskawe to the floor as Carl scooped up his phone, tucking it in the breast pocket of his false uniform shirt, then thrust a hand beneath the blanket that had covered the old man and pulled out his small digital handycam. Tuckwa glared at the camera, but Carl merely shrugged.

"You said it yourself: I'm here to get the story." He checked the camera, turned on the power, then held it up. "I'll go in first. I want to check the angles."

"The hell you will!"

But Kahleskawe already had a hold of the chief's arm, and Carl knew from experience just how much that would slow Tuckwa down. He skipped around the slow-moving pair, staying out of Tuckwa's reach. Despite the chief's intense but quiet protestations—head nurse Bethany *was* just down the hall—Carl quickly knocked-and-entered at room 217.

Room 217

"Mrs. Messing?"

No one in a hospital bed ever looked good in Carl's experience, but the woman huddled under the thin blanket had no bandages, no casts, and she wasn't crisscrossed with tubes and wires, just a single IV line running from a bag hung beside the bed. She didn't move when he came in, though, or look at him when he spoke, merely stared at the TV hanging from a bracket on the far wall. Carl moved closer, camera held low, shooting from the hip, trying not to freak her out.

"Mrs. Messing?"

She gazed toward the television. The sound was off, leaving the screen a silent pattern of moving colors, but her eyes were unfocused and blank; she only faced the TV because the bed was aimed that way. Carl wasn't sure whether her stare was the result of shock or whatever was running through that IV line, but he didn't think the liquid in that hanging bag would explain the smell.

The clean scents of trees, grass, and healthy soil—what Carl disparagingly thought of as *mountain air*—had faded quickly as he'd moved into the hospital, the elevator and corridors permeated with the chemical smell of the industrial cleaners universally favored by those combatting infection, bacteria, and the spread of germs. Part of Carl's mind had registered the hospital smell as comfortingly familiar: Cherokee didn't smell anything like Boston, but he'd spent enough time in emergency wards—both following stories and as a patient—that the antiseptic scent had been like a little slice of home.

The air surrounding the Messing woman, however, held a different tang, a sour bitterness one might have mistaken for body odor, or the miasma of bacteria trapped and built up between folds of flesh long unwashed, but Carl knew differently. That scent had come from his own skin at the hospital, then from his sheets for weeks after, every time he woke, thrashing and grunting, from dreams of his ordeal in Maine. He'd gotten very good at pretending that had never happened, to the point that even now he had no conscious thoughts of his own experience; but a small part of his mind knew he was pretending, and it was that small part that told him Mrs. Messing was *not*.

The stink of fear sweat could be washed away, but it always returned. At least for a while.

Is this why Tuckwa eventually agreed to this? Carl wondered. *If she's catatonic, then she won't—*

With a birdlike twitch of her head—as if he'd startled her, or snuck up on her somehow while standing still—she looked at him, eyes focused and aware.

"Who are you?"

Her voice was almost shrill, and her words were fast, and he realized she'd gone from flat and out of it to the edge of panic in less than a heartbeat. *She reacts like this to me*, he thought, tamping down his smile before it broke loose, *wait 'til she sees the Cherokee Butcher come through that door.*

"Good morning, Mrs. Messing. My name's Carl Spaberg, and I'm working with the police."

Technically true for the first time since he'd arrived in North Carolina. There was a mirror on the wall across from the bed, beside the mounted TV, and beneath it a small counter with a sink and cupboards. Carl bustled to the sink and set the handycam on the counter aimed toward the bed. It *might* get Kahleskawe entering the room, but it would *definitely* capture Messing's reaction, and the video was of high enough resolution that even with this wide-angle shot he'd be able to pull and blow up stills without losing much detail. He ran his fingers under a quick burst of water to cover his actions, then moved to the foot of the bed, where he'd be at the edge of the shot and not obscuring her face.

"I know you've been over this before, Mrs. Messing, but could you tell me what happened to your family? In your own words?"

He might not have time for even a partial interview before Tuckwa came through the door, but simply asking the question would get it all to the forefront of her mind. Whether she actually told him anything or not, that should be enough to prime the pump and help kick off the massive reaction he wanted. She'd go absolutely bugfuck when she saw the old man.

This, he thought, *is going to be great!*

Her round eyes looked hunted, and though she'd been pale before, what color she'd had drained away at his question, leaving her the unnatural white of sun-bleached bone.

"But the others didn't believe me," Messing whispered. "Why should you be any different?"

"Oh, I'm not like those others," Carl said, trying for a gentle smile. "I'm only interested in *you*. In what *you* have to say." *And I'm not a police chief looking to pooh-pooh your* Methuselah with a straight razor *story.*

Thinking of Tuckwa protecting his great-grandfather, it suddenly occurred to Carl that he'd been in the room for almost a minute, and there was no sign of the chief and his charge. A splash of ice water landed in his stomach.

Shit! Did Tuckwa turn around as soon as I came through that door?

Images of the chief lifting the old man back onto the gurney and hustling it up the hallway toward the elevator filled his mind. He'd seen how deftly the chief had returned the bag to the feds at the press conference; was he standing here now, holding a bag of his own as his story rolled out the back door?

But even as he debated abandoning his shot at getting the survivor's story—a worthy exclusive in and of itself, better than the *Mirror* deserved—and running out after the escaping chief, the door opened. Tuckwa entered, arguing over his shoulder with the old man currently clinging to the crook of his elbow like some slow-talking barnacle.

"You don't need to do this. We can just—"

"However I got here," Kahleskawe interrupted, in those clear, high tones he could manage when he tried. "I am here, and I should do this thing because I can."

On the bed, Margaret Messing twitched. For an instant, Carl thought she'd recognized the voice and was already starting her meltdown. When she merely turned toward the door with a darting, birdlike movement, he realized it was the same reaction she'd had to his own appearance. But Chief Tuckwa had entered first, screening her view of Kahleskawe. Once he stepped aside—

Rather than the chief stepping aside, his great-grandfather moved around him to face the woman in the bed. "Good morning, young lady." The old man had slipped back into his careful, quiet voice, coaxing rather than haranguing.

"Are you working with the police too?"

Tuckwa glared at Carl, instantly catching the question's implications, but Kahleskawe simply shook his head.

"No." He reached up, eyes still on Messing, to pat the chief's shoulder. "I am merely this little buck's great-grandfather. My great-grandson, he thought you might like someone to talk to. Someone better at *listening* than his uniformed people."

"I don't know what to say, really," she said. "I . . . uh . . ."

"Then, if you like, I can talk. I can tell you stories of what things were like in the old days—and I can tell them very well, for I was there." He shambled to the chair by the head of her bed. "Or, if you don't want to talk, or to listen, I can just sit, and be there whenever you *want* to talk. I am very good at sitting. At home I sit, sometimes for hours, my great-grandson too busy to visit or call . . ."

Tuckwa sighed and rolled his eyes. Messing caught the gesture, and Carl thought she almost smiled. "It might be nice to have a little company," she said as Kahleskawe turned to lower himself gingerly into the bedside seat.

That ice water in Carl's belly had frozen solid. *This is all wrong!*

She'd started out as wary of the old man as she'd been of Carl, but that had begun fading almost as soon as Kahleskawe spoke. Where was the explosion of fear? Did she not recognize—

"Hey, Mrs. Messing?" Her gaze shot toward him and she flinched back from his sudden step forward. He was probably blocking his own shot, but didn't care. "Don't you—I mean, do you recognize this man?"

She glanced at Kahleskawe, then immediately back to Carl, as if afraid to let him out of her sight.

"I mean, at all? Don't you know who—"

"All right, Spaberg." Tuckwa started forward. "You had your—"

"Don't you know who he *is*?" Carl said over the chief. Messing's eyes widened at his raised voice, and she shrank back as much as she could, penned in by the head of the bed and the wall behind her.

"That's enough." The chief *wasn't* raising his voice, but there was iron in it, a warning Carl ignored.

"*Look* at him! Look now! He did it, didn't he? You can say it, you don't have to be afraid."

"I said—" Tuckwa began, his voice finally rising, head nurse's orders be damned. But this was Carl's chance—his *one* chance—and it was slipping away.

"*Look at him!*" Carl thrust a finger at Thomas Kahleskawe's ancient face. "Isn't he—isn't that—"

Tuckwa grabbed his pointing arm, but Carl wrenched free. Messing writhed away, trying to get as far from Carl as possible but unwilling to leave the safe haven of her hospital bed, clinging instead to the folded-down bed rail as she hung off the far side, almost defying gravity.

"That's the man who murdered your family! Isn't it? *Isn't it*? Isn't he—"

Messing suddenly whipped toward him, flinging words at Carl. "*She looked like me!*"

"What?"

"She looked like me!"

Tears streamed down her face and it was all the reaction Carl could have hoped for, but it was aimed at him, not Kahleskawe, and what she was saying—

"Nate was crawling, trying to get out of the bathroom. I saw him, called to him, and then *he* saw *me* and screamed for me to run! And then he got up and blocked the door, and she was right there inside! She looked right at me! She stabbed him and just let him fall, but she didn't even look at him, just at me, and I saw her, and she was *me*! Same clothes, same face—*how could she have my face?*"

Kahleskawe held out a weathered hand, not to restrain or control, simply offering a lifeline. She clasped it between both of hers and pulled him closer, jerking him half out of his chair with manic strength.

"She killed him and she had my face. What if he thought it was me?" She was crying, sobbing, the complete opposite of the semi-catatonic mask she'd worn earlier. "She killed the kids, and she killed him, and she looked like me. What if he thought it was *me*? What if they *all* thought it was me? *What if Michael and Michelle thought it was me?*"

Then her words were gone, washed away in a torrent of tears. Kahleskawe added his other hand to the pile between them and she pressed her face to his knuckles, weeping into them as the old medicine man murmured words in more than one language, but all in a tone of comfort and understanding.

Carl was staring, wondering *How did this all go so fucking wrong?* when something clicked around his right wrist. A foot struck the inside of his left ankle, spreading his stance wide as a hard hand pressed between his shoulders, and he smacked face down on the foot of the hospital bed.

"You're under arrest for the kidnapping of Thomas Kahleskawe." There was satisfaction in Chief Tuckwa's voice. "Which will get us started. We'll figure out what do about *this* mess later."

The other handcuff *snick*ed around Carl's left wrist. "You have the right to remain silent."

A hand gripped Carl's shirt, hoisting him to his feet.

"If you give up that right, anything you say can be held against you in a court of law."

"Wait a minute! *Wait*, dammit!"

Carl's shoulders were pulled back while his hips were thrust forward, keeping him off-balance but on his feet as Tuckwa, ignoring his protests, steered him easily toward the door. Behind them, the old man comforted the lone survivor of what Carl already thought of as *the Mile-High Murders*.

"You have the right to an attorney."

The camera still sat on the counter, wide-angle shot capturing everything, but the only thing that footage proved was that the Cherokee Tribal Police Chief knew how to execute a textbook arrest.

MONDAY

Gingerbread Girl

Teresa Gray ran.

Her books tried to bounce against her back, but she'd stuffed a sweatshirt down into her pack as a cushion, tightened the straps, and her stride ate up the two miles between the school bus stop and home. She could have been dropped off much closer—something Mom had pointed out when Teresa'd started this, then again after that little Kanoska kid, and *again* after Lily. Teresa'd just promised to be careful and gotten off at the same faraway stop she usually used.

Teresa was thirteen—almost—and already captain of her track team, where she was faster than everyone. Even the fourteen-year-olds. She still had another year at the junior high, but coach said if she kept at it, she'd dominate girls' track when she got to high school.

That annoyed her: her current team was coed, but the high school had a girls' team and a boys' team; it wouldn't be fair, coach had explained, to expect girls to keep on competing with boys at that level. But Teresa was faster than all the boys now, and saw no reason not to continue the trend. So, she'd gone to Mom and explained her plan to run home from the faraway bus stop every day, even after track practice.

"So, what?" Mom had said. "You planning on running on the boys' team in high school?"

"No," Teresa had answered. "I'm gonna be *captain*."

She had better than a year until she got to high school, better than a year to be faster than kids who were already old enough to drive. So, despite Mom's concerns, she ran. The kid being killed right by his house did creep her out, and she'd *known* Lily. But that little kid had been *little*, and Lily was in the woods at night. Besides, Teresa was faster than all the other kids, she was faster than her coach, and she'd be faster than any wandering weirdo.

Up ahead, thunder rolled.

Mom's gonna like it even less if I'm running home in the rain.

Teresa Gray ran faster.

On a Rail

Carl had been arrested before—he considered it almost required for really hard-hitting reporters—but the lawyers usually sprang him after a few hours. Carl spent the afternoon and night in that cell, contemplating what had happened in that hospital room. It annoyed him to no end that everything Margaret Messing had said supported Kahleskawe's Spearfinger theory, and he wasted some time trying to figure how the old man might have gotten to Messing and primed her for an act that would make Carl look stupid. There *had* to be a logical explanation for the whole thing—he just had to find it.

Whatever way he looked at it, though, his big comeback story seemed fucked six ways to Sunday.

Strangely during all this, Dianne Nelawe never came to the cell to meet him.

He'd been in the Cherokee station house for more than twenty-six hours before Tuckwa had dragged a chair to the bars and straddled it backward.

"My great-grandfather says to let you go."

Carl nodded. "Your great-grandfather is a sterling individual, full of wisdom, intelligence, and compassion."

"I've been trying to talk him into pressing charges."

"Yeah, well, you're you."

"See, here's the thing: him pressing charges would be easier on me, but I don't *need* it. I caught you red-handed committing a major crime against an Indian within the Qualla Boundary. That means a federal prosecution, probably spearheaded by Special Agent Howard, and he don't like you any more than I do. Matter of fact, after that press conference, I think it would make his day, finding out he'd have the chance to fuck up your life."

Carl felt a growing dampness above his lip and under his arms. This was *way* bigger than some trespassing beef or crime scene violation. Tuckwa was right—again, damn him. His story was fucked, but *he* could be *more* fucked. He forced a grin.

"But who wants to put a smile on that smarmy bastard's face, right?"

Tuckwa's lips twitched. "The enemy of my enemy is my friend."

"Hey! I—"

"But you'd still be here for a while, and I want you gone. So, you're gone."

Carl squinted. "I'm . . . What?"

"Gone. I've been on the phone with a Maxwell Beerman, up in Boston."

"Sounds like a happy asshole, doesn't he?"

"Once I explained the situation, he didn't sound happy at all. There's a ticket waiting for you at Asheville Regional. You're in Cherokee two hours from now, we're going the federal route, with your confession to me, your own recording—you left your camera in Mrs. Messing's room, we made a copy—and the testimony of those two boys you stole the ketamine from, who realized what happened this morning and came in to apologize to my great-grandfather for being tricked by you. It'll be long and drawn out, but at least I'll get to see you miserable. You can thank my great-grandfather for encouraging me to go the quick route. Your car's outside. Get in it and go."

He stood and unlocked the cell.

"And don't think you can just skulk around out there. You got a big mouth and white skin. People already know about yesterday. You might as well be holding up a big neon sign."

Carl didn't move. "You used official channels to disseminate that information, of course."

"Smoke signals. Now get the fuck out of my town."

~~**~~

He drove straight to his motel, calling the *Mirror* on the way. According to Max's annoyingly cheerful PA, the editor-in-chief was, "Out of the office for the rest of the day, sorry!"

He was on his own.

He was packing quickly when someone knocked on his door. Praying it was anyone but Barry—what fun the prick was going to have with *this*—he opened the door to an angry-looking Ben, from Cherokee Tribal EMS.

"Ben? What are—"

Ben held up a hand. "Save it. We know what you did to Mr. Kahleskawe. *And* you fucking *stole* from us."

"Hey, I *did* give you guys two hundred—"

"Save it, I said. I'm only here 'cause when we brought him home from *you* kidnapping him, Mr. Kahleskawe asked us to bring you a message. I said I would, but I don't like it. He wants you to stop by his place on your way out of town. If I were you, I wouldn't. We all know what you did. People want to fuck you up. You should go while you can. But I told the old man I'd deliver the message, so . . ."

He turned and strode away. Carl simply grabbed his stuff and speed-walked to the rental before anyone else he didn't want to see stopped by. The sedan roared to the lot exit, where Carl jammed on the brakes and sat. Debating.

Right led south, back into town, where he'd take Route 19 east for the sixty-mile drive to Asheville Regional. He'd finally get the fuck out of this armpit of a town.

But left took him north, practically past Kahleskawe's trailer. The old man *had* sort of gone to bat for Carl. What did he want to say?

But if Tuckwa even thinks *I'm going to Kahleskawe's, I could wind up a feature on* Strange Disappearances.

Of course, the construction site that had started it all was up in Kahleskawe's neighborhood. He could always say he was looking for a last set of pictures or something.

But really, he thought. *Is it worth risking federal prosecution—or maybe a frigging scalping—just to hear what a crazy old man who believes in Cherokee fairy tales has to say?*

He sighed. "Aw, fuck it."

He turned left.

Is that thunder?

The Cookie Crumbles

Teresa checked the sky.

Thunder's really *close now, but I don't see any clouds.* She remembered the distant sounds of the dynamite the mall construction crew had used until last week, the far-off air horn followed by a rolling boom. *That had sounded like thunder. I wonder if they've started construction agai—*

"Teresa?"

Lost in thought, Teresa had run right past her own mother standing at the roadside. She slowed, turned, and jogged back.

"You come to pick me up because of the thunder?"

Mom nodded, beckoning, but something struck Teresa as a little off—and she put her finger on it just as she drew near the woman standing on the shoulder with one hand tucked behind her back.

"So, where's the car?"

Mom lunged, eyes flashing gray in the sunlight, hidden hand flying out wide. Primed by her thoughts of dead kids and roadside weirdos, subconsciously tipped off by the missing car, Teresa's athletic reflexes kicked in and she managed to turn her forward jog into a quick backward hop. Mom's arm whipped

That's not Mom!

in an arc between them, something long and sharp *swishing* through the air. The hop lifted Teresa's throat up and out of danger, but the blade, black and straight-razor thin, *snicked* through her backpack's right shoulder strap, slicing the flesh beneath. Gasping at the sudden pain, too surprised to scream

That's not Mom!

Teresa landed from the hop already spinning and taking the first step into her sprint. She could outrun the other kids, she could outrun her coach, and she could damn well outrun this weirdo by the side of the road who was definitely *not* her mom, and—

And the backpack, falling loose from the cut strap, swung around with her spin, slipped off her other shoulder and fell, slamming into her shins, cutting her feet from under her. One hand tangled in the still-whole strap, the opposite shoulder burning with pain, neither arm moved to catch the road when it rose up. She'd opened her mouth to scream, but her front teeth shattered against the tarmac, her nose crunched flat, and all she managed was a bubbling wail. Nearly unnoticed in all this, a stonelike grip encircled her ankle. Then it was dragging her backward, flipping her over to stare up at the cloudless sky and the hand with a forefinger like a foot-long obsidian blade hovering in it.

Told You So

Carl entered the curve at speed. He'd managed to shake off the old man's bullshit, and had come back to his senses in that cell, but this thunder *wasn't* . . . well, thunder. It wasn't *acting* like thunder: it was starting and stopping in continuous short bursts. And though his view to either side was hemmed in by the forest through which the road cut, his view of the wide cloudless sky was unhampered. He'd opened his window to listen, but it quickly became so loud, even with wind and road noise, there was really no need.

Seriously, what the fuck?

Then he came out of the curve into a straightaway, and there was a kid, a girl, falling to the road in front of a figure. The figure—a woman, he saw, short and kind of chunky, in jeans and a sweater—dragged the girl back by an ankle and stepped over her, long knife held high.

Holy shit! It's her!

Part of Carl wanted to grab his camera and start shooting wild. The car was moving fast, but he just *might* catch an image that would help him rise out of tabloid hell. On the other hand, this was a murder in progress, and it clearly *wasn't* spindly old Thomas Kahleskawe—but God *damn* it, it *should* have been! That Tuckwa would be giving Carl the *I told you so* rather than the other way around was simply infuriating! Carl mashed the accelerator.

The blade started down.

You ruined my story! Take that, you bitch!

Carl's left front bumper caught the woman full on the hip.

With a metallic *crunch* and sharp *boom*, the car jolted sideways. The world went white and Carl's nose was flattened as the airbag deployed. He stomped the brake and the sedan whipped in a half-circle, tires screeching, skidding to a halt even as he beat the rapidly deflating bag down out of the way. It took seconds that felt like minutes, but eventually he was looking through the windshield again. The sedan had swung pretty far around, and he recognized the patch of land straight in front of him as the place the kid had lain when he'd come around the bend.

But where is she? he thought groggily, staring at a small backpack lying abandoned on the dusty shoulder.

Thunder rumbled, close and loud. The door behind him suddenly jerked open. He spun in his seat—just as a young girl, her face a mask of blood, flung herself into the backseat.

"Christ! Are you okay?"

"Naw maw maw!"

What the fuck was that? Cherokee? "English, kid!" he shouted over the incessant rolling thrum. "*Are you okay?*"

She sat up toward him, and he saw her smashed nose and bloody lips. *Jesus, she looks like Stallone at the end of* Rocky. Her mouth opened wide to enunciate, and he flinched. Carl loved the motto *if it bleeds, it leads*, but was used to seeing it through the filter of the camera, and his gorge rose at this sudden up-close view of gums filled with shattered bleeding stubs.

"Naw mah mom!"

When he still looked blank, she pointed out the passenger's side window, shrieking a single imperative requiring no teeth.

"*Go! Go!*"

A figure strode from the trees, holding the long blade he'd last seen plunging toward his new passenger. But while he could have sworn the woman he'd struck with his car had been short, plump, and wearing a blue sweater, he saw now she was tall and wore a traditional Cherokee dress and long braids, both the color of slate.

And as she walked, the thunder rolled.

It took him a moment to understand. From where he sat, he could see the crumpled left fender of his rental, the metal torn and out of shape, and he was pretty sure that headlight was a thing of the past. But if that was the woman he'd hit, she was walking just fine, wasn't even limping—shit, she hadn't even dropped the knife.

She's crazy, Carl thought. *Or on something, something bad, to shake off being hit like that.*

She charged. The thunder *roared*. Carl felt the earth shake, felt each footfall—and as she drew nearer, he saw that blade wasn't a knife, but a long, sharp finger.

Thomas Kahleskawe suddenly spoke up in Carl's reeling mind.

When she walked it sounded like rolling thunder, and her skin of stone turned aside their arrows. The world is bigger than what you see every day, Carl Spaberg. Older, too. You need to open your eyes and see.

And deep down within himself, that little piece of Carl that had recognized Margaret Messing's fear sweat, that had always remained aware the "Monsters in Maine" story had really happened, that understood that *X-Files* shit was sometimes real no matter what day-to-day Carl had managed to convince himself, lifted its head and looked the rest of him right in the eye.

Told you so.

"Fuck this place." He pumped the gas, reaching around the drooping mushroom of the expended airbag to jam the shifter into park and fumble for the keys. "I hate North Carolina. I'm going home."

He'd seen all right. And heard. This lady—this *thing*—sounded like thunder, and she'd practically ruined his rental and come out of it without a scratch. She was barely five yards away when the engine hiccupped to life.

I've been fighting Kahleskawe and he's been right all along. Fuck it! It's time to get the hell out of Dodge, bring in a tactical unit—shit, maybe the army—and—

He dropped the shifter into drive and hit the gas. The car lurched in a tight left half-turn. Carl, grip on the wheel beneath the airbag tenuous at best, was thrown toward the passenger's seat. She was right there, swinging her arm, her hand—her *finger—*

Glittering cubes of Safe-T-Glass showered the interior when the rear passenger's window shattered. Screaming in unison with the terrified girl, he stomped on the gas again, wrestling with the wheel as the engine roared, struggling to keep the car out of its left turn and stay on the road, gaining speed, but far too slowly. He heard metal grinding and the *flud-flud-flud* of a shredded tire and recalled the *boom* in the middle of that crunching impact

Shit! Blowout!

This was crazy. He was on the run from a myth, a local boogeyman Cherokee moms probably used to keep their kids in line. But he'd seen it, hit it with his *car*, damn it, and—he checked the rearview—yup, it was still coming.

Can I outrun her?

The girl in the back certainly thought so, beating his seat and shouting, "*Go-go-go!*"

He checked the speedometer: 20 miles per hour. He bore down on the gas, but the banging from what was left of the tire shook the vehicle so hard he nearly lost control, and he was already tiring just from trying to hold a straight line. He checked the rearview again.

Barely outrunning her. But if Jason Voorhees and Michael Myers are any indication, I'll be exhausted long before she is.

He was fleeing back around the bend, away from Kahleskawe's and toward town, but he'd never make it that far. He racked his brain for somewhere to run to, but all he'd seen were outlying homes, and if she really *were* stone, no regular house door would stop her.

Fuck! We're scr—Wait!

There was one place he *knew* was close by, and knew the way there, and *maybe* he could swap to a better vehicle. If he was very lucky.

He checked the rearview again. The Spearfinger thing was slowly losing ground, but still coming, like a guided avalanche. He tightened his grip on the steering wheel and tried to speed up. He was going to need a little lead time.

Fight or Flight

The yellow crime scene tape was in view when the sedan bucked and died. The shredded tire had quickly fallen away, but steam had been pouring from the cracked radiator in ever-increasing clouds. Then, a half mile back, the engine had begun knocking like an angry cop: a blown head gasket. Carl rolled out of the still-steaming vehicle shaking his hands, trying to regain circulation—he'd spent four minutes clutching the wheel in a death grip, bare rim trying to send them careening off the road.

"Why we spop?" said the girl—Lisa, he thought she said her name was. She'd yammered at him the whole way there, and though he'd tried to ignore her, she *had* become easier to understand with practice.

"It's dead, Jim."

"Wha? Hey—Whea you go?"

Ignoring her—he'd honestly hoped she'd have passed out by now—Carl jogged to the huge dump truck beside the excavation, then paused to listen.

Rolling thunder, somewhat distant, but getting closer.

Fuuuuuuuck . . .

He scrabbled up into the truck's cab. Ignition slot empty. Nothing under the seat or tucked above either sun visor. A worn shovel and pickaxe lay on the passenger's-side floor; he shoved them aside to check under that seat as well.

Nothing.

"Shit!"

It may not have keys, but it does have gas, and ten big, thick tires. Thank God it's an old Mack rather than one of those huge Cat things, and already aimed at the road, or I'd be screwed.

He nearly soiled his pants at a sudden pounding on his door. He looked out the window, then cranked it down. "What?"

Lisa stood beside the truck: she refused to pass out, had mostly stopped bleeding, and apparently objected to being left behind.

"Waa abou me?"

"What about you?"

She flapped her good arm in an obvious *What the fuck, dude?*

He pointed. "Go hide in that pit, or maybe in the backhoe. I'll try to lead her away, then you try to flag down a car, all right?"

She looked like she might have argued, if she'd had the strength. Or the teeth. She tottered off toward the pit, moving pretty well, he thought, compared to Spearfinger's other victims.

And if old Spearfinger finds her, that's just a little more time for me to get the fuck out of here.

He unrolled his little traveler's toolkit he'd grabbed from the rental's glovebox, set a screwdriver into the ignition slot, and gave it four hard shots with the hammer. He pressed the clutch, pumped the gas, and twisted the screwdriver. The big engine rumbled to life. He checked the diagram on the shift knob, worn but mostly legible, and shoved it into first gear. It wasn't smooth by any means, but he got the huge truck juddering and grinding toward the road.

I might not have my CDL, but at least I can drive stick. Nothing fancy, just keep it rolling. And avoid running into a tree or anything.

He looked around, but didn't see Lisa anywhere. *Kid's a good hider*, he thought. *She'll be fine.* But as he rolled toward the road, listening to the engine, trying to figure out when to shift the behemoth, he pictured the girl: mouth bleeding, wide-eyed with terror but still feisty, jumping in his car and screaming *Go! Go!* Flapping her arm in a *What the fuck?* He shoved the images aside, focusing for a moment on the growing thunder.

That's the thing to think about, Carl old buddy. You ran right into her, at speed, wrecked your car and she's still coming. This is un-fucking-believable! You've got to get the hell out of here and get the story out there. The story *is the important thing, and you can't get the story out if you're dead.*

But somehow, this was different. He shifted into second and forearmed sweat from his eyes.

You cover the news. You get the story—and you can't get *the story if you're* part *of the story.*

Those were words he'd once lived by, back when he'd been a real reporter, for a real newspaper: you can report the news or you can make the news, but you can't do both. The reporter remains an observer, untouched.

But aren't I part of the story already? I became part of it when I fucked up and got arrested in the hospital. And I hit *that thing! Saved a victim! Other reporters are going to want to interview* me *now. And* this *story . . . After what happened with "Monsters in Maine" . . .*

"Fuck!"

He was fast approaching the road, and just like back at the motel, he had a choice to make: left, away from the chasing monster, or right, and toward her.

You fucked up last time, buddy boy. If you'd just gone away like Tuckwa wanted, you wouldn't be in this mess. You'd be driving through the mountains, halfway to Asheville Regional by now. Left, baby; turn left and go the fuck home.

But, the thought came, *parts of your car are all over the road right beside that kid's school bag, and her blood's all over your back seat. You could be in Norway when they find the body, but if that kid turns up dead, Tuckwa and those two BIA stooges are going to make sure you get the chair, or the needle, or whatever they do in this God-forsaken state.*

"Ah, shit."

Besides, piped up that *X-Files is real* part of him. *That little girl is counting on you.*

"Oh, shut up," he muttered, though he couldn't hear himself over the booming thunder as, uncertain just what the hell he was doing, he swung the big truck ponderously to the right.

Truckin'

He was just working the truck into third gear when he looked up and saw Spearfinger coming straight for him, middle of the road and pounding along like a stone machine. Despite himself, Carl almost grinned: he'd wrecked his rental, but he *had* knocked the liver-stealing legend off the road, and this truck was about ten times the size of the sedan—and half loaded.

"Let's see you shake *this* off, you bitch!"

He goosed the accelerator. The engine roared, and the big truck slowly gained speed.

This is like driving a tank, and it's not like I'm a deft hand at the wheel. She dodges me, I can't turn this thing around for a second try.

But as he rolled west and she pounded east, her stride changed, slowing a bit and angling just a touch to his right, and Carl felt hope.

The way she fucked up my ride, she must be made of stone through and through. She's got to be one heavy bitch!

And with that much weight—what, five hundred pounds? Seven? A thousand? What did a human-sized statue weigh?—packed into such a relatively small object, that meant she had a ton of inertia—maybe literally—driving her toward him. If he could get the truck to her before she managed to overcome it . . .

His foot was already to the floor, but he grit his teeth and *willed* the huge vehicle forward, jockeying the wheel to compensate for her slightly changing course. They drew closer

. . . closer . . . and she threw up a defensive arm just as he lost sight of her around the tall, steel hood.

"Yeah!" he screamed. "Fuck up *my* story?"

There was a jolt in the steering wheel and seat, a horrible tearing of metal, and the passenger's side window actually shattered. The truck swerved and he fought to straighten it, listening for the *thud-thud-thud* of the triple-axeled Mack rolling over this anthropomorphic speed bump.

Nothing but engine noise and the sound of ten tires rolling on the tarmac poured in through the broken window. He looked to his right, following the sound, a little dazed but marveling that he'd hit her so hard the glass had shattered—and a gray head and arm lurched in through the opening, the limb swinging in an open-handed slap. He shrank back with a cry. Most of the slap fell about a foot short, but he screamed as the tip of that spear finger of hers *whick*ed through the meat at the top of his shoulder.

Now he knew why the window had shattered and the big vehicle'd swerved: she'd managed to at least mostly dodge the truck and leaped up to jam her non-spear hand through the glass to grab the window's edge. He heard the *plonk-plonk* of her setting her stone feet against the truck, probably on the step below the door, and she withdrew a bit, both hands gripping the window frame, long, razor-sharp forefinger cutting deep into the door's armrest. Her gray face twisted into a stone snarl as she dipped and the cab rocked; it didn't take a genius to see she was setting herself for a serious lunge through the window. Then she'd hack and slash and that would be all she wrote for Carl Spaberg, ace reporter. He'd die right there, or maybe in the crash, but either way, his liver would wind up in the belly of the beast—and it was that thought right there, just the incomplete, incoherent flash of that fate in his mind, that fueled his own desperate lunge. Throwing himself flat on the seat, wounded shoulder screaming almost as loudly as Carl himself, he grabbed the passenger's side door handle and yanked, just as the squaw from hell began her surge into the cab.

And he stomped the brake.

The antilock ratcheted loudly against his foot as the truck's nose dipped, not quite managing to skid as the tons of dirt and rock back in the bed tried to come up into the cab to say hi. The unlatched door flew open, the surprised-looking U'tlun'ta sticking through the open window to the waist, a dog halfway through a pet door. Whatever she weighed, it was too much for the old truck's hinges. The door snapped off and skated down the road in front of the rapidly braking truck, taking Thomas Kahleskawe's stone ogre with it.

Inhaling sharply at the pain from his shoulder, Carl struggled upright behind the wheel, managing at the last moment to shove in the clutch and avoid stalling the engine. Ahead, Spearfinger rolled to a stop. She still seemed unharmed, trying to stand immediately, but was hampered by the door she now wore as a sort of apron, the upper rim of the window frame mashed in against her back from the weight of her rolling over it.

The Cherokee hunters trapped her in a pit, Carl thought, feathering the gas and easing out the clutch, clinging to the wheel like a drowning man. *I wonder if they ever tried a deadfall.*

She saw the rolling mountain of metal coming and tried to rise, knees slipping on the inside of the battered door, but he steered straight for her. He felt the first bump and hit the brakes, but felt the second bump before the truck actually stopped. Stalled. Stood silent.

Carl sat a moment with his forehead pressed to the steering wheel, collecting himself. He tested his right arm; the shoulder hurt like a mad bastard, and he likely needed stitches, but he wasn't crippled. Still, he favored it a lot as he climbed down from the cab.

Crushed beneath the four big rear driver's-side tires, Carl's mother lay dying in the road. Her nose was flattened, eyes bulging and mouth leaking blood from internal injuries. He couldn't see how she was still alive, with a thirteen-ton truck parked right across her chest, but she was. Struggling weakly, labored breaths puffing blood into the air and across her face, she lifted an entreating hand toward him.

"*Carl . . . help me . . .*"

Her entreating hand had one extremely long finger, straight as a ruler and sharp as a razor. The one thing Thomas Kahleskawe had said U'tlun'ta simply could not change.

"I'll help you. Just a minute."

Feeling not quite a part of everything, as if watching someone else playing him on TV, Carl walked around the truck to the place where no door barred him from the passenger's side seat. When he came back around to where his mother lay pinned beneath the truck, she saw the worn pickaxe across his shoulder, and her eyes widened.

"*Carl?*"

Carl flexed his wounded shoulder, testing the pain. He'd seen hard guys, knew he wasn't one of them, but thought he could manage, at least for a while. "You know? If you'd looked like anybody else right now, I'd probably be trying for some kind of interview."

He heaved up the pick and took a practice swing. What was it Kahleskawe had said? *She held her heart in her spear-finger hand to keep it safe.* And even through whatever she was using to disguise herself, he could see the other fingers of that hand were wrapped around something. The hand was pressed to one of the huge tires now as she struggled against the great weight, face twisted into a grimace of rage.

"But there's no way *this* story wouldn't just make things worse for me, and Mom and I have never gotten along. Not since . . . Well, it's a long story. Suffice it to say, this . . . this may actually be therapeutic."

Then, looking past the face, into the furious eyes of the thing, he raised the pickaxe high. "Fuck you, you story-fucking bitch. Whatever you are."

The pick came down.

Breaking Up is Hard to Do

It took a while; his shoulder hurt almost more than when she'd cut it, and blood sleeved that arm down to his fingers. Hitting U'tlun'ta's wrist hadn't worked; she'd simply moved it out of the way again and again. But she couldn't move her shoulder, and once he'd shifted targets, things had progressed pretty well. She'd begged awhile in Mom's voice, which had quickly grown rather annoying. Once the shoulder had begun to crack, though—and that had been strange, seeing his mother's shoulder chip and split like shale—the arm hadn't flailed as much and she'd been wailing in a deep, James Earl Jones voice, shouting words he hadn't understood. That had made things easier.

When the arm finally separated, both it and the suddenly silent figure beneath the truck shimmered, and Mom's tear-streaked face became one of stone, hard and immobile. It had just occurred to Carl that he should run back to what was left of his rental and grab his camera—his newsman's instincts demanded he get *something* out of all this—when the figure suddenly crumbled to gravel. The arm crumbled too, leaving behind two chunks of obsidian: a foot-long blade, sharp as a razor, and, buried in the mound that had been the hand, a smoothly rounded knot, half again the size of a chicken's egg.

"Well God damn it."

Our Hero?

Carl received twenty-one stitches from head nurse Bethany herself, while handcuffed to a hospital bed and wearing an ice pack on his forehead.

The handcuff was thanks to Chief Tuckwa, who'd caught Carl trying to slip back into town driving a thirteen-ton vehicle carrying about eight tons of payload. He'd started out angry when he recognized part of a crime scene cruising down the road, grew furious when he saw it was Carl behind the wheel, and become apoplectic when Lisa slipped rather woozily from the cab. The ice pack was from Officer Ahoka, who, when ordered to cuff Carl by the apoplectic chief, was either so affected by his boss's mood or overcome with his own feelings at seeing the poor abused girl, he'd shoved the reporter down on the hood of their cruiser with such vigor Carl's forehead had left a shallow dent.

Lisa—he'd since learned her name was *Teresa*—had tried to speak on Carl's behalf, but since no one else could understand the poor kid any better than Carl had, nobody listened. He'd sat in the hospital bed (quite calmly, he thought) receiving threats of prosecution from Chief Tuckwa, then the two stooges (Special Agent Howard doing all the talking while Special Agent Fine stood in the background cracking his knuckles until Carl told him it could lead to crippling arthritis in later years). Then Tuckwa took another turn. The chief was mid tirade when he was called from the room, much to Carl's relief. Ten minutes later Carl found out why: a dental specialist had been called in to take a look at the child's broken teeth, and she could understand the girl perfectly.

Carl suddenly had a new appreciation for his own dentist's habit of waiting until Carl's mouth was immobilized to try to start a conversation.

Two hours later, Teresa had (through her new interpreter) told everyone who would listen how Carl had saved her from someone who looked like her mother but was definitely *not* her mother—a story close enough to Margaret Messing's, Carl thought, to at least give Chief Tuckwa the creeps. He'd led the killer away while she hid, she'd said, then returned to drive her to the hospital. Carl was still in his hospital bed, though *sans* handcuffs, and the two stooges had come by to apologize. Special Agent Fine even asked his opinion on Aspercreme, for when his knuckles started to bother him.

There had been no sign of the chief since the revelation; apparently, he couldn't bring himself to be in the same room as Carl. The reporter's official statement was taken by a very apologetic Officer Ahoka.

". . . and when you hit the brakes, the door she was hanging from just . . . just came off?"

Carl shrugged his good shoulder. "It's not my truck, Officer. I can't say *what* kind of shape it was in before I borrowed it."

"*Stole* it."

Carl shrugged again. "Extenuating circumstances. Had to save the girl. You understand."

Ahoka stared at him a moment. Then: "And after the door came off, she just ran off into the trees?"

"Yup. I mean, she'd already been hit by my car. Must have been hurt pretty bad. Then, with the door . . . She was just lucky to still be moving."

"About that." Ahoka referred to his notes. "You say you hit her with your car—"

"The kid corroborated that."

"—and though Teresa's blood was in the back seat . . . there was no blood *on* your car, either on the hood or any of the bits scattered in the road. Or where we found what was left of the door."

He looked up from his notebook.

"How do you explain the lack of blood, Mr. Spaberg?"

"I don't," Carl said. "You do. That's your job, Officer."

He could have tried to explain that the stones and gravel on and under that door in the road *was* the body from which they were hoping for blood spatter evidence, and that their killer had simply crumbled and was even now blowing away as dust in the wind—all but that obsidian finger and heart, which were currently hidden in his luggage back in the replacement sedan; they were going to make a terrific paperweight and letter opener set when he got back to his office. But he remembered how his "Monsters in Maine" story had been received and held against him—was *still* being held against him—and kept his lips tight shut.

That evening, the door opened and Thomas Kahleskawe tottered into Carl's hospital room.

"Sorry it took so long to get here. My great-grandson hasn't come by to see me, so I had to find another ride."

Carl raised his eyebrows. "Amazon?"

The old man shook his head. "Heard your story about her running off into the trees. Went to see for myself. Found some of my great-grandson's people sifting through some gravel piled around a truck door in the middle of the road. Got a ride with them. They said the gravel must've fell out the truck when it bumped over the door." He shook his head again. "Didn't look like it fell to me. That woulda been kind of splashed around. This looked like maybe some big rock just . . ." He spread his hands. "Fell apart."

It was Carl's turn to shrug. "Dunno. Not my truck."

Kahleskawe smiled, a baby's smooth grin. "You saved the girl. You did well."

"Not that well. I mean, I got a story, but . . . not the kind I wanted. The kind I *needed*." Carl frowned. "You're the only reason I was even out there, you know. The ambulance kid said you wanted to tell me something. What was it?"

The old man looked pleased. "Doesn't matter now. I was going to ask you to tell Crawley to send out a replacement right away."

Carl's jaw dropped. "*You* know *Crawley*?" His confusion at his ancient editor seeing a story down here when Carl himself had not suddenly disappeared. "*You're* how he knew to send me down here! *You're* his *tip*!" His mouth worked without sound for a moment as his mind raced—*What is this, the* really *old boys' network?*—then: "You mean I'm only down here in the *first* place because *you* asked for me?"

"Not exactly. When I suspected U'tlun'ta had been released, I called long-distance from my great-grandson's office and asked Crawley to send his best investigator."

"Well," Carl said, puffing out his chest. "Like I said—"

"He said his best was busy, so he was sending you. But that's okay." He squeezed Carl's shoulder with a warm grin. "You did well."

The ancient medicine man's insane grip, crushing in on Carl's twenty-one fresh stitches, forced all the air from his lungs. Carl writhed, making only the occasional agonal grunt as Thomas Kahleskawe tottered back across the room and out into the hall. The door had closed behind him before Carl could manage three panting syllables.

"He . . . said . . . *what*?"

Weekly World Mirror: Headline
CHEROKEE BUTCHER EVADES CAPTURE!
Authorities floundering!

—Cherokee, NC

Following his incredible nose for news, this reporter made his way to Cherokee, North Carolina, scene of last week's Soco Creek Construction site massacre: five men slaughtered in a foundation pit, tools in hand. Local police "investigated," blamed eco-terrorists, and back-burnered the case; yours truly smelled an ongoing story. By the time the *Mirror* had boots on the ground, another murder had occurred, just as bloody but even more shocking: eight-year-old George Kanoska, butchered in his own backyard. The next day, the killer savaged another child, Lillian Ghigooie, age twelve.

"And how," you may ask, "did they know the killings were linked?"

Though local police and regional FBI attempted obfuscation, your faithful news hound (me, of course), quickly ferreted out the truth: the livers had been cut from each of the seven victims, taken by the killer for reasons unknown.

Black market sales? Satanic ritual? Cannibalism? While local and federal authorities pondered, the Cherokee Butcher—named by this reporter during an historic press conference—struck again, slaying three vacationers in one fell swoop: Michelle and Michael Messing (age 9) and their father,

Nathan Messing (age 36), leaving the mother, Margaret Messing (age 34), alive but in a state of deep shock.

Unable to get anything from their lone witness, Cherokee Tribal Police Chief Charles Tuckwa called upon this reporter for help. Using interviewing techniques honed sharper than the Butcher's knife through years of investigative work, this reporter obtained a physical description of the evil perpetrator.

The Cherokee Butcher was a woman.

Description in hand, police began a street patrol in search of The Butcher, hoping to apprehend the monster before she struck again. Taking part in the patrol—I felt it was my duty, dear readers—I happened upon the roadside assault of one Teresa Gray, age twelve. Recognizing her attacker from the description, this reporter leapt to the girl's defense. The battle was long and hard fought, but the Butcher finally escaped into the trees.

After the thrashing dished out by Spaberg—at one point the escaping killer was struck by a rental sedan (sorry, Hertz!)—authorities are monitoring local hospitals while combing the North Carolina forests for the body of the serial killer.

As the last person to have seen the monster, this reporter thinks they're going to come up short.

By Carl Spaberg, Ace Reporter

Regarding the full details of the story, all serious book offers will be considered.

(I'm looking at you, Random House!)

Author's Note

So, you read the whole thing—unless, that is, you're one of those people who skip to the end of a book to see how it turns out. There are names for people like that, some of them not very nice, but you won't catch me using any of them here. I figure you paid your money, so this is your book you're holding. You can read the end first if you like. You can start in the middle and read every other word if you want, no one's stopping you.

But remember: you have to live with yourself.

This is the part where I get to tell you the story behind the story, sort of pre-answering that question every writer hears: *"Where do you get your ideas?"* This one came from a book. Actually, two books. *Actually*, two books and a character.

I'll explain.

The first book: *Wicked Creatures* is an anthology from the New England Horror Writers *now*, but back in January, 2021, it was just a submission call, the *idea* for a book looking for stories about monsters. I was determined to offer them one. I started a changeling story, but they were looking for *short* stories, and this tale wasn't cooperating, insisting instead on being far longer than what they wanted. I turned away from that story to write a gremlin story . . . which didn't cooperate either. Closer, though, so I tried to edit it down. I managed to get it short enough, but only by editing the story right out of the story.

Big nope.

In despair, looking for inspiration, I plucked a book from my reference shelf, which brings us to—

The second book: *The Vampire Slayers' Field Guide to the Undead*—that hefty tome we see Carl pushing aside during his library visit—is a real book, written by a real person, Shane MacDougall—though you may know him better as his alter-ego, Jonathan Maberry. It's a doorstop of a reference volume, briefly informing on hundreds of undead/supernatural creatures from all around the world—perfect for finding a monster those editors over at the NEHW might never have heard of. On page 384, I found a quick paragraph covering the Cherokee myth about U'tlun'ta, "a bloodthirsty ogress who slaughters people and eats their livers."

Bingo! I was hooked.

I started the story of the return of U'tlun'ta, deciding to make it an investigation. Specifically, an investigation by an outsider; someone local likely would have heard about Spearfinger, and be familiar with the territory, and I wanted someone totally unfamiliar. I started out writing a Bureau of Indian Affairs agent, but I pictured them having too many resources I know nothing about, plus I kept having scenes from *Thunderheart* (1992) rolling through my head. I tried a state cop, an agent of the North Carolina State Bureau of Investigation (SBI), but the Qualla Boundary *does* fall under federal jurisdiction. I started looking into who would have original jurisdiction for a series of homicides on reservation land, even going so far as to email the question to the North Carolina SBI—yet *another* watch list my research has probably landed me on. Suffice to say, when Carl notes that the Qualla

SPEARFINGER

Boundary is a jurisdictional tangle, from the layman's point of view, that isn't poetic license.

I realized I was doing an awful lot of research for a simple short story, and I needed to rein that in a bit and do more actual *writing*. What I needed was an investigator with minimal resources, not from the area, who just might have an issue with believing all this mumbo-jumbo, all of which brings me to—

The character: Carl *fucking* Spaberg.

This is the third story I've written about Carl, and by far the longest—yup, this was yet another failed attempt at writing something for *Wicked Creatures*. The problem was, I *know* Carl. I know his backstory (which is actually more complicated than even *he* thinks), his flaws, and his motivations. I also started out a few years ago writing him as a villain; he's not a particularly nice man, and fairly self-absorbed, and that makes him a lot of fun to write, which might have something to do with him popping up in my head now and again.

When I realized what I was writing was going to be a) *far* too long, and b) much more about Carl than the monster he was hunting, I set it aside to try again. My fourth attempt, "Wood you Love?" was finally short enough. The NEHW liked it, and it does appear in *Wicked Creatures*—it's a good book, you should check it out. I shouted "Success! Huzzah!" and quickly returned to Cherokee, NC, and U'tlun'ta.

And Carl.

Freed from the mental restraints of *trying to keep it a short story*, I got to play with Carl a little, adding to the page a few bits of his backstory and some background characters that had formerly only taken up space in my head (including some new stuff; Carl's relationship issues with his mother were a complete surprise!). He reads a little nicer here, though whether that's me wanting people not to hate him or simply the result of seeing his actions from *his* point of view rather than from the outside—he's essentially trying to frame an old man and a police officer because he feels it makes a compelling story, which is pretty fucking despicable when you get right down to it—I can't tell.

What I can tell is, I liked running around inside Carl's head for a while. He's selfish, pushy, bigoted (through caring too little about everything rather than caring too much about the wrong things), his self-confidence cup doth runneth over, and he couldn't tell a scruple from a nutria if one ran out of the dark and bit him on the ball sack. He's the opposite of me in so many ways—not just the self-confidence, though that's a big one—I find I really enjoy being his mouthpiece in the world; this man who so desperately wants not to believe in the supernatural things the universe has to show him, but, at the end of the day, just can't help it. I plan to write more of Carl's tales whenever they come to me, so I hope you enjoyed reading about him as much as I enjoyed writing about him.

And if not? I'm sorry. But hey, at least *I'm* having fun!

—*Rob Smales*
August 8, 2022

About the Author

Rob Smales is the author of dozens of short stories, the collection *Echoes of Darkness*, the novellas *Friends in High Places* and *LaundryLegs*, and identifies as a dad, writer, editor, and postal worker—in that order.

To find out more about him, you can look him up on Facebook or check out his website at www.RobSmales.com.

About the Author

If you liked Spearfinger, try Friends in High Places!

He just wanted friends

He pestered them day after day to be considered one of the guys, but they didn't want anything to do with him. They ignored and made fun of him, ditching him at every opportunity, but Tommy wouldn't take the hint.

They came up with a plan to drive him away.

It was only a harmless prank

In order to be accepted, Tommy would have to pass an initiation and face his worst fear. They were certain he'd chicken out, but he accepted the challenge.

That's when it all went wrong.

If only they hadn't left him

The ambulances wouldn't have come.

The police wouldn't be asking so many questions.

And maybe Tommy wouldn't still be following them.

Also by Rob Smales: LaundryLegs

Old Mr. Ross didn't believe in LaundryLegs. He thought the monstrous centipede was made up by his wife—a joke to scare their kids. But after his wife's death, Mr. Ross finds himself face-to-face with the creature.
Or does he?
Stricken with grief over the loss of his wife, and fearful of his looming mental decline, Mr. Ross begins to doubt his own sanity. Is the monster in his basement real? Is it an alcohol-fueled nightmare?
Or is he losing his mind?